"There's

Olivia glanced at Andrew sharply. "And what is that?"

He stayed silent a moment, then turned to face her. "We could get married."

He saw utter shock on her face. For a few heartbeats, there was silence except for birdsong.

Finally she spoke, and her voice was grim. "Andrew, marriage is forever. Do you really want to be yoked with a woman like me?"

Whatever reaction he might have expected, it wasn't this. He was genuinely bewildered. "A woman like you? What do you mean?"

Despair crossed her face. "Handsome men don't marry plain women."

"That's the second time you've said that. It bothers me."

"Well, it bothers me too." She looked severe. "You would regret marrying me, Andrew. Trust me."

Did she really think she was the plainest woman on the settlement? Did that really mean so much to her?

He slowed his chaotic thoughts down and tried to imagine things from her perspective: unmarried, unlikely to *get* married, compelled to earn a living as a single woman. Did she long to change that?

Living on a remote self-sufficient homestead in North Idaho, **Patrice Lewis** is a Christian wife, mother, author, blogger, columnist and speaker. She has practiced and written about rural subjects for almost thirty years. When she isn't writing, Patrice enjoys self-sufficiency projects, such as animal husbandry, small-scale dairy production, gardening, food preservation and canning, and homeschooling. She and her husband have been married since 1990 and have two daughters.

Books by Patrice Lewis

Love Inspired

The Amish Newcomer
Amish Baby Lessons
Her Path to Redemption
The Amish Animal Doctor
The Mysterious Amish Nanny
Their Road to Redemption
The Amish Midwife's Bargain
The Amish Beekeeper's Dilemma
Uncovering Her Amish Past
The Amish Bride's Secret
An Amish Marriage Agreement

Visit the Author Profile page at LoveInspired.com.

AN AMISH MARRIAGE AGREEMENT

PATRICE LEWIS

If you purchased this book without a cover you should be aware that this book is stolen property. It was reported as "unsold and destroyed" to the publisher, and neither the author nor the publisher has received any payment for this "stripped book."

Recycling programs for this product may not exist in your area

ISBN-13: 978-1-335-23007-2

An Amish Marriage Agreement

Copyright © 2025 by Patrice Lewis

All rights reserved. No part of this book may be used or reproduced in any manner whatsoever without written permission.

Without limiting the author's and publisher's exclusive rights, any unauthorized use of this publication to train generative artificial intelligence (AI) technologies is expressly prohibited.

This is a work of fiction. Names, characters, places and incidents are either the product of the author's imagination or are used fictitiously. Any resemblance to actual persons, living or dead, businesses, companies, events or locales is entirely coincidental.

For questions and comments about the quality of this book, please contact us at CustomerService@Harlequin.com.

® is a trademark of Harlequin Enterprises ULC.

Love Inspired
22 Adelaide St. West, 41st Floor
Toronto, Ontario M5H 4E3, Canada
www.LoveInspired.com

Printed in U.S.A.

Thou shalt not covet.
—*Exodus* 20:17

To my husband and daughters,
my greatest earthly joy.

To Jesus, for His redeeming grace.

To God, who has blessed me
more than I could possibly deserve.

Chapter One

Olivia Bontrager slowly woke up from a deep sleep. She had been dreaming about her father, specifically that awful time he had to be transported to the hospital. The sound of the ambulance siren still echoed in her brain.

Her room was unfamiliar, and it took a few confused moments to realize she was no longer in the rural farmhouse in which she'd grown up. That was far away in Pennsylvania. She had embarked on a new life now. She was, for all intents and purposes, alone. Her mother had died when she was a toddler, her sister was off in parts unknown and her father…well, her father's recent passing was the impetus to sell the family farm and move to the newish Amish settlement outside the tiny town of Pierce, Montana. It was a chance to start fresh, away from the grief.

The morning light shining through her bedroom window heralded another warm midsummer day. She gazed out at the pale pink clouds dotting the sky. The dream had been a disturbing one, the kind that lingered even after awakening. She felt the sharp, familiar sting of loss as she realized she would never see her father again in this life. At least he was no longer in pain.

She blinked and stretched, still half-asleep. Then she frowned. Was she still dreaming? The sound of the siren could still be heard. Was it a real ambulance, way out here in the midst of the Amish farms?

Except... She snapped fully awake. It wasn't a siren she heard. Was it a cat yowling? A wild animal? A bird? She got up, unconsciously noticing she had slept long past her usual time. She snatched her bathrobe and dragged it over her long nightgown, then emerged into the messy main room of the tiny cottage she was renting. The sound seemed to be coming from outside her front door, a mewling waa-waa. Oddly, it sounded almost like...a baby.

She strode for the front door and yanked it open. The beauty of the early-July morning poured in—sunshine and birdsong and fresh air. She didn't even notice the car seat on the doorstep until a thin wail emerged from it.

It *was* a baby! What was a baby doing on her doorstep? It took a moment longer to notice the small suitcase next to the carrier.

Olivia stared at the infant. A baby. A baby with black hair, clenched fists and a red face, dressed in a thin onesie with a teddy bear motif. A tiny human, something she never thought to have for herself. The one thing she was never able to give to her father before he died...

She shook her head. This wasn't her baby. So whose was it?

The infant wailed afresh. Olivia wasn't familiar enough with babies to guess its age, but it was certainly tiny. Two months old? Three months? She wasn't sure.

She lifted the handle of the car seat and brought the infant indoors, then placed the carrier on the kitchen table, staring at it. The jolt of movement momentarily silenced the infant, who opened its dark eyes and looked around.

Olivia stared, entranced. A tiny maternal part of her stirred to life with a thrill. It was a cliché to leave a baby on a doorstep, and usually signaled abandonment. As a spinster among a church of famously fertile cohorts, she stood out due to her unmarried state. She blinked back sudden tears. All his life, her father had wanted grandchildren. Her older sister never married and had left the faith years before. Olivia herself had been so busy caring for the man who had raised her after her mother died that she had never found the time to be courted.

A sneaky part of her wondered if this was a baby she could keep. Or was that legal?

Suddenly, she remembered the suitcase. Olivia dashed outside, seized the valise and brought it in. After unsnapping the lid, she pawed through a plethora of supplies: diapers and bottles and powdered formula and baby wipes. And...a note.

A note. She seized the sheet of paper and scanned it. Her gut clenched.

It was from her sister Adele. "The baby's name is Helen," the note read curtly. "She was born on May 1. I discovered I'm not cut out for motherhood, so she's yours. I met a wonderful man and I'm moving to Europe with him. *Danke*, dear sister."

May 1. The day her father died.

May 1. That would make the infant just a touch over two months old.

And Helen. That had been their mother's name. Olivia had only vague memories of her mother, but Adele remembered more, though she seldom mentioned their deceased parent.

Olivia crumpled the note in a sudden fury. Her older sister had done nothing since childhood but cause their father grief. He had never remarried and had done his best to raise his daughters to be *gut* Amish women, with the help of various aunts.

But Adele had rebelled from the start and taken off for the *Englisch* world at eighteen during her *Rumspringa*. She had a habit of dipping back into Olivia's life whenever she needed a bit of stability, usually to cool down after a bad relationship.

But—*a baby*! How could she abandon her own child?

Little Helen screwed up her face and began emitting thin wails while her tiny fists clenched and her face became red.

Olivia's fury faded and panic took its place. She had no experience with babies, having never had any younger siblings and being too involved in geriatric care to participate in any babysitting activities. Was the baby hungry? Tired? Bored? Irked? Stressed? What?

She pawed through the suitcase again and found the powdered formula she'd spotted earlier. Hands shaking, she scanned the directions, then dashed toward the kitchen sink. She measured some tepid water into a measuring cup. She spilled a little of the formula as she used the little scoop to add the powder to the water. Meanwhile, the baby's wails increased in volume, creating a stressful backdrop to Olivia's steep and abrupt learning curve.

In the middle of this frantic activity, she heard a knock at her door. Her sister! Who else could it be but Adele? Olivia dashed past the wailing infant and yanked open the door, prepared to give her sister the dressing down she deserved.

But it wasn't her sister. It was a perfectly strange man. An Amish man with dark brown hair and cheerful blue eyes, nice-looking in a comfortable, stable sort of way. He wore a tool belt. Olivia drew up short, startled.

He smiled. "*Guder mariye*. I'm here to—"

"Do you know anything about babies?"

His smile dropped and he looked surprised. "What?"

"Babies!" She resisted the urge to seize him by both his suspender straps and yank him into the house. "I've just had my sister's baby dropped on my doorstep, and I don't know what to do! Do you know anything about babies?"

He peered inside and saw the crying infant. Uninvited, he walked over and gently probed the baby's diaper. "He's wet," he pronounced. "That might be one of the reasons he's crying."

"It's a *she*, not a *he*." Olivia pawed once again through the little suitcase and yanked out a tiny disposable diaper. "Is this what you need?"

"What *I* need?" He raised his eyebrows.

She flushed. "Can you change her diaper?" she pleaded. "That way I can continue making up a bottle."

"*Ja*, sure." Looking amused, the man unsnapped the straps in the infant's car seat and lifted the baby. "I have younger brothers and sisters, so I've changed my share of diapers. She's tiny. How old is she?"

"My sister's note said she was born on May first, so that makes her just a bit over two months." Olivia pushed a strand of hair out of her face and darted for the kitchen area again, nearly tripping over a pile of thin willow branches on the floor.

The man rummaged in the suitcase and pulled out a box of wet wipes. "Can I change her here on the kitchen table?"

"Um, how about my worktable?" Olivia turned around long enough to sweep aside a mess of pine needles and straw to one side, then jerked a couple of kitchen towels from a drawer to pad the surface. "I can't believe my sister did this to me…" she muttered.

"I'll take care of the diaper. You take care of the formula," the man said.

Relieved to be sharing the burden with someone—anyone—Olivia turned back to the kitchen counter. She closed her eyes, took a deep breath and finished mixing the formula. She pulled a feeding bottle out of a plastic bag in the suitcase, noting in passing that the man's expertise in changing the baby's diaper far exceeded her own…especially since her own experience was nonexistent.

The baby was quiet during the diapering process, and Olivia was relieved. Maybe that's all the infant needed…

"She's ready," said the man. He lifted the infant, supporting her head, and cradled her in his arms. The baby, apparently realizing her bottom was now dry, suddenly bunched her tiny hands into fists and let out another thin wail.

"What's the matter with her?" fretted Olivia. Following the directions on the can of powdered formula, she finished pouring the mixture into the bottle, capped it and gave it a good shake.

"I suspect she's just hungry," the man said calmly. He gestured toward the rocking chair, her only chair in the house besides the two chairs around the kitchen table. "Sit down and I'll put her in your arms."

Placing the bottle on the table, she sank into the rocking chair and awkwardly held out her arms for the infant. The man transferred the baby, then picked up the bottle, gave it another good shake and handed it to her.

"Just put it in her mouth, *ja*?" she said.

"*Ja*," he replied.

Olivia slipped the rubber tip into the baby's mouth, and sure enough the crying stopped instantly. She gave a sigh of relief.

Andrew Eicher pulled one of the kitchen chairs into the living room, closer to the rocking chair, and dropped into it. "Obviously, this is new for you."

"*Ja*. What was your first clue?" The woman leaned her head back and sighed. "I found the baby on my doorstep a few minutes before you showed up. Apparently, my sister dropped her off."

"Your sister *abandoned her own baby*?" He was shocked to his core at the callousness of the action.

"*Ja*. See that note on the table? Read it."

He scanned the note and his eyebrows rose. "Quite a sister."

"You don't know the half of it." The woman sighed again. "I've often wondered if she went astray because she didn't have a mother's guidance. Our mother died when I was two and my sister was five. She was always a rebel, and this is just her latest escapade."

"Yet apparently, *you* turned out fine."

"I listened to our father's guidance. Adele never did." He saw pain lance her expression and guessed she might have just recently lost her father.

There was a brief silence while she looked down at the infant, an unfathomable look in her eyes. She was a tall, rawboned woman utterly lacking in beauty, but she had beautiful dark brown hair in a long braid down her back and kindly blue eyes. She was attired in a rather ratty bathrobe over a long cotton nightgown. She exuded strength and character despite her panic over the infant.

After a moment she raised her head and smiled at him. She had a nice smile. "I'm Olivia Bontrager, by the way. I'm so sorry I yanked you into the house, but I appreciate the help."

"My pleasure. As I said, I have a number of younger brothers and sisters, so I got roped into changing diapers often enough. I'm Andrew Eicher. Your landlady sent me over to do some work on the roof."

"Oh, is that why you're here?" Olivia managed a rusty chuckle. "*Ja*, it's leaking. You can see I put a bucket under it, there." She pointed with her chin toward a pail set in the corner.

The pail was just one aspect of a room far messier than most Amish people ever permitted their homes to get. The chaos rather surprised him. Andrew wondered why she had so many materials spread around the room that looked like they should be in a barn or a garden—piles of willow branches and boxes of pine needles, shreds of bark and other debris. However, it wasn't his place to ask.

The baby gave a tiny grunt and fell off the bottle. Trying to be helpful, Andrew took the bottle and handed her a dish towel. "You'll want to burp her now."

"Burp her? How do I do that?" The panicked look was back on her face.

He suppressed a chuckle. "Here, let me have her. I'll show you." He unbuckled his tool belt and placed it on the floor, then removed his straw hat and dropped it on top of the belt. Tossing the dish towel over his shoulder, he leaned down and took the infant, hitching her over his shoulder and gently patting her back. "Especially with bottle-fed infants, it's necessary to help them get any extra air out of their gut by burping," he explained. "If you don't, they're likely to get very uncomfortable and cry a lot more."

"There's so much I don't know…"

"You're like any new mother. If you keep her, you'll learn." He paused. "*Do* you intend to keep her?"

"*Ja*. My *d-daed*—he always wanted grandchildren." She blinked hard. "But he died before he had any. If this is Adele's baby, then it's *Daed's* only grandchild. Of course I'll keep her." She took a deep breath. "It just means I have to get some mothering lessons, that's all."

He admired her in that moment. Whoever this odd, gangly woman was, it was no small task to raise an abandoned infant, niece or no niece. Her words were brave, and he realized she had no idea what lay in store for her as a single mother. But it was not his business to pop her bubble.

"Well, we have nothing *but* mothers around us," he replied lightly. "I'm sure any one of them would be happy to give you pointers on how to handle a newborn." He continued patting the baby's back.

"*Ja, gut* idea. I'll have to ask around. I just moved here. I'm brand new to Montana. Er, do you want to sit down?" She rose from the rocking chair.

"*Ja, danke.*" He took her seat and continued to pat the infant. He raised an eyebrow. "I can hold her if you want to get dressed," he hinted.

"Oh!" She glanced down at herself and blushed scarlet. "Um, *danke.*" She fled the room.

He chuckled and set the rocking chair in motion, still patting the infant until he heard a satisfying *braaaap*. Then he repositioned her until she was cradled in his arms.

The baby was actually darling. Her hair was almost black, and her eyes seemed dark as coffee beans. He felt a small thrill in his arms as he looked at her. What would it be like to have a baby of his own? He wasn't likely to find out anytime soon.

He leaned his head back and emitted a sigh, much as Olivia had done a few minutes ago. He wasn't married and had no prospects for doing so anytime soon. A farm, he hoped, would take the place of the family he didn't have. And—maybe—it might become the springboard for attracting a wife at some point in the future.

That was why he wanted to get this roof-repair job done early. He had an appointment with his landlord this afternoon, who'd said he might know of a farm that might interest Andrew. In fact, buying a farm was his sole goal in traveling to Montana, since farmland was too expensive back in Ohio.

Traveling to Montana also meant leaving behind the most beautiful woman he'd ever known. He had eagerly courted Sarah, who'd seemed to love him as much as he loved her—until she met someone better looking whom she claimed she loved more, and unceremoniously dumped him.

He grimaced at the memory. He was almost madder at himself than he was at Sarah. He realized now he'd been so dazzled by her outward appearance that he forgot, as the Bible instructed, to look at the inner self, the unfading beauty of a gentle and quiet spirit. Sarah, he realized in retrospect, had far more outer beauty than inner. And he, fool that he was, fell for it hook, line and sinker, until the day she callously informed him how much better looking her new beau was than he himself. Then the blinders had been stripped off…

The baby squeaked in his arms, and he jolted from his bitter memories and realized he was clenching his muscles. He took a deep breath, relaxed his hold on the infant and prayed for forgiveness—both at his own youthful folly and the anger that still stubbornly kept hold of him whenever he thought of the woman he'd wanted to marry.

In retrospect, it was a blessing from *Gott* that she'd dumped him. To be yoked for life to a beautiful but shallow woman was not what he wanted.

But his experience had left him soured on women in general—and beautiful women in particular. He had been diligently saving his money since his teenage years to purchase a farm, which would give him the opportunity to provide for a wife and children. Sarah's defection had snatched from him the future family he'd always hoped to have. At this stage, still heartsore, he couldn't even see himself courting anyone again.

And now… He looked at the infant in his arms. Now he was resigned to bachelorhood, at least for the time being. He didn't know if he would ever hold a baby of his own. So, in lieu of his role as a family man, he had taken his extensive savings and migrated west in hopes of buying that mythical farm of his dreams. A farm would take the place of a family, at least for now. Developing the land into something productive, being able to sell the fruit of his labor—that was the role he knew *Gott* had in store for him.

His only concern was that he might not have enough money to pay for a farm, even at the lower prices in Montana. It was why he was eager to find work and earn more. This repair gig on Olivia's roof was the first of his freelance carpentry work, and he wanted to prove himself capable and eager.

His lifted his eyes away from baby Helen and glanced around the room, struck anew by its messiness. What on earth was this woman doing with so much detritus indoors? Piles of willow branches, boxes containing long stalks of straw and hay, bowls of pine needles, rolls of jute, even stacks of palm leaves, which looked wildly out of place in a Montana cabin. Looking more closely, he realized there were crafting supplies among the materials: large needles with stout thread, rolls of wire, nippers and other cutting tools… He shook his head. Olivia's disorderliness was none of his business, though it jarred the innate sense of tidiness and order that had been instilled in him since birth. He wondered what she did with all these materials.

The infant in his arms gave a tiny sigh, and he looked down at her. She had fallen asleep.

Andrew felt the stirrings of emotion in him. He wasn't supposed to feel fondness for a baby he had met only half an hour ago. But the child looked so innocent and vulnerable.

What kind of mother was Olivia's sister that she could so callously abandon her own child and jaunt off to Europe with her latest beau?

Another thought struck him: he didn't know how Olivia planned to earn a living, but caring for an infant would likely put a damper on her plans. He wondered if she'd thought of that yet. If this morning had unfolded as she said it had, he doubted it.

Well, that was a benefit of being in the church. She would have lots of help whenever she needed it.

"You may not be my *boppli*," he told the sleeping infant, "but you're a pretty *boppli* just the same. I kinda wish you were mine."

Chapter Two

Standing in front of a tiny mirror hanging on the wall, Olivia shoved a hairpin through the braid she had wound into a bun. Her hair was so long that sometimes it was a struggle to secure it modestly, but today it gave her no trouble.

The small mirror was something she avoided looking into except when necessary. She had none of her older sister's exotic beauty and preferred not to have a visual reminder of that. She was plain as a crow—and at nearly thirty years of age, that put her firmly in spinster territory.

She had never known the pleasures of courtship, but she had enjoyed a warm and loving relationship with her father. For the time it lasted, it had been enough. She was strong and healthy, and it was no hardship to take on more and more of the work on their small farm so he wouldn't be overburdened. Adele was simply too flighty to depend on, and later dropped away from the church. With no brothers to help around the farm, the work simply needed to be done, so Olivia had done it.

Her father seldom spoke about his disappointment with his older daughter, but Olivia knew Adele's desertion had hurt him deeply. Ever supportive, her father had encouraged her to develop her basket-making skills so she could earn a living on her own. Olivia had never expected to get married, much less be a mother, so she had thrown herself into her specialty…until now.

Little Helen's abrupt arrival threw her for a loop. This wasn't how she'd wanted to start her new life in Montana—taking care of a niece she hadn't even known existed. The arrival of a baby disrupted the projects she had planned, including a trip to town to see if anyone was interested in carrying her wares.

She felt a flash of fury at her sister's actions. It was so like Adele to sow trouble wherever she went. It was just the latest—and most serious—of an escalating series of trials. She suspected Adele hadn't dared see her sister face-to-face because she knew she couldn't justify her decision to abandon her own child. As always, Adele had depended on her younger sibling to bail her out of trouble.

Yet a tug of latent mother-love warred inside Olivia along with the anger at her sister. It wasn't the baby's fault that her mother was a flake. But could she—Olivia, the long-standing spinster—actually adopt little Helen and become a mother? She didn't know.

Attired in a wine-colored dress and clean apron, she snatched up her *kapp* and plopped it on her head, then emerged from the bedroom to see the stranger—Andrew—holding the infant in the rocking chair, gently rocking back and forth.

"She's asleep," he remarked the moment she stepped out of the bedroom. "Should I just put her back in the car seat for the time being?"

"No." It jarred Olivia to see an Amish infant in a car seat. "Let me think for a moment..." She glanced around the room holding all her raw supplies, then—pushing aside some cattail leaves—she seized a sturdy oblong basket made of seagrass. *Perfect*.

"Let's use this." She placed the basket on the kitchen table, padded it with a towel and invited the man to lay the infant down in the makeshift cradle.

He rose slowly from the rocking chair, walked toward the table and gently tipped the infant into the basket. The baby snuggled in with a sigh and didn't awake. "Nice fit," he remarked as he straightened up. "Where did you get a basket like that?"

"I made it."

"You *made it*?" He looked at her, and his jaw dropped.

She felt a flush of pleasure at the man's obvious approval. "*Ja*. I'm an expert basket-maker. It's how I make my living. Just about everything you see in this room is something I use in making baskets."

"I just thought you were messy." His eyes crinkled with humor as he glanced around at the chaos.

"*Ja*, it's messy." She nudged a bowl of lengthy pine needles. "After I sold the house I grew up in, I moved to Montana to buy my own place, with room for a studio where I can do my work. This rental is too small. I have nowhere I can organize my raw materials, nowhere to set up a workbench. I'm hoping to find a place that will accommodate me. Meanwhile, I apologize for the mess." She glanced at the infant. "It's no place for a *boppli*…" she ended in a low tone.

"Are you sure you want to keep her?" The man's face took on a concerned expression. "I'm certain there are any number of families here on the Amish settlement who would be happy to take her in."

"*Nein*." She felt a stubbornness overtake her. "Abandoned or not, she's my *daed's* only grandchild. Besides, apparently Helen was born on exactly the same day *Daed* died—May first."

A pang of sharp grief speared her. "Is that not a sign I should keep her? He died without seeing her or even knowing she existed. He always wanted grandchildren. Now that he's gone, I could no more give away his only grandchild than I could change my eye color."

Andrew gave a half shrug. "All I can say is, your sister must have *really* wanted to dump her baby if she followed you here. Pierce is not an easy place to find, a long way from anything. I should know since I only arrived a few days ago. It's hard to believe she traveled all this way for the sole purpose of abandoning her baby."

"My sister knows I never shirk my responsibilities," replied Olivia. "I'm three years younger than her, but somehow I've always felt older. Still, you're right. The fact that she didn't even so much as knock to let me know the baby was outside makes me realize how nervous she was about my reaction to abandoning her child." She sighed. "I'm sorry, that's a lot of information. You didn't need to know all that."

He brushed a gentle finger over the sleeping baby's cheek, a gesture Olivia thought looked both tender and experienced. "If you don't mind my asking," he asked, "why don't you have any experience with babies?"

Olivia stiffened with resentment, ever sensitive to her unmarried status. But there was no mockery in Andrew's expression, only mild curiosity. She realized the chip on her shoulder was hers, not his. "I was too busy taking care of *Daed*," she said quietly. "He was ill for a long time. And I... I..." She was about to add that men weren't exactly lining up to court her, but thought better of it. "And I was just too busy to learn about babies," she ended lamely.

"I see." She could plainly make out the curiosity on his face, but he was too polite to admit it. All he said was, "Well, you're in for a steep learning curve." He bent down to retrieve his tool belt and buckled it around his waist. "I'll get started on the roof, then, unless you need me for more baby care." He quirked an eyebrow at her.

She caught his humor and smiled. "*Nein*, and *danke* for the help."

"I hope I won't wake her when I start hammering," he warned, starting for the door. "Your landlady asked me to make a number of repairs to this cottage, both inside and out, so maybe I can plan things around the baby's sleep schedule."

She smiled. "You'll have to wait until I know what that is." She liked Andrew. He was levelheaded and good in an emergency.

He nodded, plopped his straw hat back on his head and left the cottage.

Through the window, she watched as he shouldered a ladder, then leaned it against the side of the house and climbed up. He moved with the efficiency of a man used to repairs and construction. Doubtless, like most Amish men, he had been practicing these skills since boyhood.

Long ago, her father had been just as able-bodied and efficient as any other man in their church. But the slow-moving cancer had gradually robbed him of his strength, and Olivia had begun to take over the repair jobs on their small farm under her father's tutelage. She was quite handy with a hammer herself...

Speaking of hammering, the sound of vigorous banging up on the roof made her wince and glance over at baby Helen. The infant stirred in her sleep and made little smacks with her lips. Olivia watched, fascinated, as the tiny hands moved, the fingers as delicate as flower petals. The first hint of blooming affection took root. Somehow, she would manage to make it work. She would not turn away her father's first grandchild.

The banging continued. She wondered how long little Helen could sleep through the racket.

Meanwhile, she had work to do. She put a kettle on to make herself some tea and scrambled some eggs for a hasty breakfast. All the chores associated with moving to a new place would have to wait while she adjusted to her new responsibilities.

However, some things couldn't wait. She needed to clean up her little cottage to make a respectable, healthy setting for an infant. She thought she would be able to take her time to find a house, a leisurely search for a place with enough room to spread out her basket-making materials, and perhaps a small place where she could keep chickens and a garden.

But if she planned to keep Helen, then she had a new sense of urgency to find her permanent home. The mess she was living in right now was no suitable place for a baby, even one too young to move around.

More immediately... She looked at the empty bottle Andrew had set on the kitchen counter. She needed formula, and diapers, and clothing, and whatever else was necessary to care for an infant.

Most of all, she needed advice. Who could she turn to for help here in her new home, besides the man banging on the roof overhead?

Conscious of the sleeping baby in the cottage below him, Andrew tried to hammer softly, but such a thing wasn't possible.

As he worked on the roof, he thought about the extraordinary events Olivia had experienced in the last hour. Honestly, dropping a baby off on a doorstep—could there be a more storybook cliché? He couldn't decide if the woman was brilliant or stupid in her decision to keep her sister's abandoned infant.

He knew a woman back east in his church who had been tragically widowed shortly after her first baby was born. It was a huge struggle for her to raise the infant on her own for that first year. She later married someone she may not have been wholeheartedly in love with, but he was a *gut* man willing to be a father to her fatherless child. In the end it had worked out and they were very happy, but Andrew remembered the struggles she'd faced during that lonely year of widowhood.

And now, it seemed, he was about to witness a similar situation unfurl. He knew Olivia didn't have a clue what she was getting herself into. At least the young widow in his old church had mentally prepared herself for motherhood throughout her pregnancy. Olivia didn't have that advantage.

But hey, it was none of his business.

Except—he had to admit, the baby was darling.

He grimaced and banged the roof with unnecessary vigor, thinking about Sarah. He hadn't forgiven her for dumping him so unceremoniously. The anger lingered. By now he had hoped to be a father, holding in his arms his own son or daughter, not the abandoned child of a strange woman's unethical sister.

It took him a few moments to realize he was clenching the handle of the hammer as unpleasant memories washed over him. He took a deep breath, prayed for forgiveness and surveyed the roof with a professional eye.

The farm he hoped to buy would take the place of the family he'd hoped to have. It was a lot to ask of a parcel of land, he knew, but if that was what *Gott* wanted him to do, then *Gott* would provide that perfect piece of land. The search would begin this afternoon, when his landlord was going to take him to see a place that had come up for sale.

In the meantime, he was resigned to staying in the bunkhouse the Millers had cobbled together in an outbuilding on their property. Right now he had two roommates, both single like himself. The Millers had big hearts, and knew young men needed a place to stay when first arriving at the Montana settlement, as well as help finding jobs. Andrew was determined to prove himself in his work.

More focused, Andrew finished repairing the leaking section of roof and descended the ladder, then ratcheted it down and placed it on the ground. As he straightened to remove his tool belt, the thin wailing of a crying baby hit his ears. He smiled and knocked on the door.

Olivia, looking frazzled, answered with the baby in her arms. "I can't decide if she's wet or hungry," she said without preamble.

His brow furrowed. "Are you sure you're up for this?"

"What choice do I have?" she snapped, then scrubbed a hand over her face. "I'm sorry, that wasn't called for. But I'm determined to keep her, if for no other reason than to honor my father."

"My *mamm* always said, 'Check the diaper first,'" he advised helpfully.

She nodded, pivoted and strode toward the table where the towel still padded the surface. Laying the baby down, she probed a finger into the garment. "*Ja*, you're right. She needs changing."

"Want help?"

"Well, *ja*, of course, but I figure I need to learn to do this on my own. Maybe you can supervise."

His admiration for her ratcheted up. He lingered nearby as she fished a diaper out of the suitcase, then instructed her as she accomplished the task. When the baby was clean and fresh, Andrew was rewarded with a big smile on Olivia's face. "That wasn't so bad."

"You'll get used to it too." The woman was as plain as an iron pot, but he had to admit her smile gave her face a certain sweetness. "If she still fusses, you'll have to feed her again."

"I did it before, I can do it again." Olivia lifted the baby in her arms and cradled her, making a kissy-face at the infant. "I'd like to say she looks like my *daed*, but she doesn't. She looks very much like my sister. That means she'll likely grow up beautiful. I just hope she doesn't grow up rebellious."

"Your sister is very beautiful?"

"Ja." Her expression hardened. "We were very unequal in that department. *Daed* always said Adele looked like our *mamm*, but she sure never acted like her. I'm sorry," she said again. "I seem to be dumping a lot of stuff on you, things you don't need to worry about."

"I wonder…" He hesitated. "You're going to need a woman's advice on how to care for this baby. My landlady is the same as your landlady, Anna Miller. She's a very motherly sort. She's had a bunch of babies and now has many grandchildren. Anna might be a *gut* woman to show you the ropes. I have an appointment with her *hutband* shortly to go look at a piece of property. Do you want me to walk you over to see Anna?"

"Ja, bitte!" He saw relief on her face. "I'm

going to need a crash course in mothering, so hopefully Anna can be my teacher."

"I can take you right now. Will that work?"

Olivia looked at the infant in her arms. The baby was making anxious noises that fell just short of crying. "I'm getting the impression she's hungry again. Can you wait while I feed her?"

"*Ja*, sure. Here, I'll hold her while you prepare the bottle."

"*Danke.*" She handed him the infant and dashed for the kitchen.

Andrew gently hitched the baby up over his shoulder and began pacing the room, dodging the piles of organic debris. The movement quieted the child, though he sensed the reprieve was temporary.

He watched as Olivia prepared the bottle of formula with impressive efficiency. She didn't seem nearly as frazzled as before. "It helps that she's not crying, *ja*?"

"*Ja*. I'm not feeling as stressed. *Danke* for holding her."

Within a few minutes, the bottle was ready. Olivia armed herself with a dish towel and sank into the rocking chair. Andrew handed over the infant.

"Ahh." She set the chair in motion as the baby began feeding. "No crying this time."

"I can see how this will interfere with your

work, however." He gestured toward the collection of basket-making materials.

"*Ja.*" She sighed. "I'm going to have to figure this out. It's not like I can hire anyone to take care of her for me, since that rather defeats the purpose of keeping her in the first place."

He pulled over the same kitchen chair he'd sat in earlier and seated himself opposite. "I think one of the reasons *Gott* made a pregnancy last nine months is because it takes that long to mentally prepare for motherhood," he quipped. "You bypassed that whole stage."

"*Ja*, and since I never thought I'd be a mother at all, I never bothered learning the basics."

"Why would you think that?" he asked, puzzled.

She leveled a look at him. "Isn't it obvious?"

"*Nein.*"

"You'd think differently if you grew up with a sister as beautiful as mine."

Comprehension dawned. It was obvious Olivia thought she wasn't pretty. Which, he had to admit, she wasn't. Not like Sarah had been. Not like Olivia's flaky sister, either, evidently.

"Looks aren't everything," he murmured, then resisted the urge to clap a hand over his mouth. He hadn't meant to say that out loud.

"Perhaps not, but they're helpful to…to have

babies." Olivia's cheeks flushed scarlet, and she ducked her head to look down at the infant.

For some reason Andrew was charmed. Having been snared by Sarah's innate coquetry, then burned by her desertion, it was refreshing to meet a woman who had no illusions about her appearance.

"If you're going to go over to Anna Miller's," he offered after a few moments' silence, "you might want to pack a diaper bag. I can do it, if you like."

"I don't have a diaper bag. Why don't you grab one of those baskets?" She inclined her head toward a pile in a corner.

He walked over and examined the selection. She really was extraordinarily talented. The baskets were jumbled in a careless pile, but every last one was a thing of beauty. He chose a medium-size piece and brought it over to the kitchen table, where the suitcase of baby things was located.

"At least your sister gave you some supplies," he ventured, pawing through the suitcase and choosing a selection of diapers, wipes, a spare outfit and a couple of small towels. "There's an extra bottle in here, so you can make another bottle of formula at Anna's place."

"Ja, danke." Olivia examined the bottle being consumed by the baby. "I think she's not far from being done."

He finished packing the basket as he watched her slip the bottle from the replete baby's mouth, then hitch her over her shoulder for a burping. "You learn fast," he commented.

"I don't have a choice, since I've made the decision to keep her." Olivia rose from the rocking chair. "If you don't mind carrying the basket, I'm ready to walk over to Anna Miller's."

"She's going to get heavy if you carry her everywhere you go," he warned, seizing the basket and following Olivia's determined figure out of the house. "But it's not like a stroller will work on these gravel roads."

"That's one of the things I'll ask about," Olivia remarked, taking long strides. "I need baby lessons. I hope Anna is interested in teaching me what she knows. After all, I can't depend on you all the time, though I'm more grateful than I can say for your help this morning."

"Bitte." He chuckled. He liked Olivia's dry sense of humor. "I'm just glad I was around to help."

He had a feeling she was going to need a lot of help in the days ahead.

Chapter Three

With a dry and fed baby over her shoulder, Olivia walked with Andrew down the gravel road deeper into the Amish settlement. By now, she knew the cluster of farms and small holdings lay three miles outside the tiny Montana town of Pierce, and that no *Englischer* lived among the church members. But the settlement wasn't a town. It had no stores or other businesses. It was simply a widely scattered cluster of church people from various places back East who had purchased properties on what used to be an enormous ranch.

"I like it," she murmured, gazing at the dense coniferous forests interspersed with fenced pastures and fields of crops.

"You like what?" said Andrew.

"The landscape. It's very pretty."

"*Ja*. Different from Ohio, where I came from, but I agree. It's pretty."

"Why did you move?" she inquired, curious

about the man who had been so helpful during this morning's unexpected arrival.

He was silent a moment, and she glanced at him. His face had a shuttered expression, and she got the impression that whatever he'd left behind was painful.

"Farmland," he finally said, with a firmness she didn't quite understand. "I've been saving since I was a youngie to buy my own farm, but they're too expensive in Ohio. Prices out here are cheaper."

She nodded. "*Ja*, I understand that. I don't want an entire farm, since I'm not a farmer, and especially now if I have little Helen to raise, but I'm looking for a place with room for at least chickens and a garden." She shifted the baby to the other shoulder. "It shouldn't be a problem to purchase something since I sold my *daed's* place."

"Where was that?"

"Pennsylvania."

"So we're both starting out new here, *ja*?"

"*Ja*." She smiled. "You said you were new too. How long have you been here?"

"About a week. The Millers made over a building on their property as a sort of bachelor quarters since a lot of young, unmarried men are arriving and need a place to stay until they find something more permanent."

"And you said you're looking at a farm this afternoon?"

"*Ja*, Eli Miller said a family had to move back East for a family emergency. They're selling lock, stock and barrel, including livestock and even furniture. Right now someone else is boarding their animals."

"Wow. Must have been a bad emergency." Having lived through her own beloved father's ill health, she sent a silent prayer toward the unknown family.

She shifted Helen once again. For such a tiny infant, she was surprisingly heavy. "I can't wait to get better acquainted with everyone. It was difficult to leave the church I'd grown up in, but I just couldn't stay after … after *Daed* passed away." She blinked hard.

"So many people are moving west for so many different reasons," he agreed, then pointed ahead. "Look, that's the Millers' place. That outbuilding over there is where I'm staying. *Komm*, let's see if Anna is home."

The Millers' place looked surprisingly established, considering the Amish settlement was less than ten years old. Evidently it was laundry day, since the outdoor clothesline held sheets, quilts and freshly washed clothes. Olivia could make out the figure of Anna on a side porch, swinging the handle of a manual washing machine. The older woman raised an arm and waved. Olivia and Andrew waved back.

She shifted Helen once more to the other shoulder. As they approached, Anna descended the stairs from the porch, wiping her hands on her apron. Andrew spoke. "*Guten tag*, Anna. I brought Olivia with me. She needs your help."

"Help in what way?"

"I'm in a bind," admitted Olivia. "I was gifted with a baby from my sister this morning." She patted little Helen's back. "She literally abandoned this little one on my doorstep. Andrew showed up to do some repairs to my cottage roof during a moment I was panicking about what to do. He suggested you might be someone who can offer me new-mother advice."

Anna's face held a comical expression of shock at this brief explanation. "You mean this baby was dumped on you with no warning?"

"*Ja*. My sister has always been…wild. I suspect she knew I wouldn't balk at taking in her own child, which I'm guessing is why she didn't even bother to knock. I just lost my f-father a couple months ago, and he died without ever having the grandchildren he so desperately wanted." Olivia blinked back tears. "This *boppli* was born on the day he died, according to my sister's note. I feel obliged to keep her, but I'm clueless about what to do. Can you help?"

Sympathy swamped the older woman's face. "Ach, *ja*. What a situation. *Komm* in, *liebling*, and let's give you some mothering lessons."

It was exactly what Olivia had hoped for. She looked over at Andrew. *"Danke. Vielen dank."*

He handed her the basket of baby supplies and touched the brim of his hat. "I'll be off, then." His gaze shifted to Anna. "Is Eli around? He was going to show me that piece of property."

"*Ja*, he's in the barn." Anna gestured as she opened the door to the house to usher Olivia inside.

The inside of the home was tidy and cozy, just like Anna herself. The older woman motioned toward a rocking chair. "Sit, child. I imagine you're tired, holding that baby all the way over here."

"*Ja*, I am." Olivia settled down with a sigh. She was gratified to see little Helen had fallen asleep.

"Now, tell me everything that happened." Anna settled her wider form in another chair.

Olivia told her everything—her father's recent passing, her trip out here with the intent of purchasing a home for herself, even the reasons behind her single status. There was something about the other woman's motherly face that encouraged Olivia to spill her guts. Some instinct told her the information was safe in Anna's keeping.

"So that's why I'm determined to keep this baby," she concluded. "But that's also why I have so little experience with babies. I wasn't even sure how to change a diaper until Andrew showed me."

"Well, let's tackle things one at a time," suggested Anna. "First, since strollers won't work on the gravel roads we have out here in the settlement, I suggest you use a sling. You'll find it will save your back and arms from getting so tired, and the *boppli* will benefit from being close to you, especially since she's a bottle baby."

Anna rose, rummaged around in a hall closet and emerged with a length of cloth. "I used this when my own were babies, so it's seen some hard use. This is how you use it." She demonstrated how to don the garment, then carefully picked up the sleeping baby and slipped her into the sling, tightening the strap until the infant was snug against her chest. "Babies are happiest when they're being carried," she said. "You'll find she won't fuss nearly as much, as long as she's not hungry or doesn't need a diaper changed. Here, you try it."

Olivia's awkward attempts to imitate Anna's graceful movements resulted in a crying baby, but then something amazing happened. Once little Helen was snug in the sling against Olivia's chest, she ceased her wailing and actually looked around. Olivia was delighted.

"*Gut*. That's step one," approved Anna. "Next, diapers. If you go into town, you can buy some cloth diapers and diaper wraps at one of the stores. Cloth diapers make much more sense because you don't have to keep buying disposables again and again." The older woman also gave advice on making diaper wipes, washing diapers and other practical matters.

"Whew," whistled Olivia at the end of two hours, a diaper change and another bottle. "This has been a crash course in motherhood if I've ever seen one."

"*Ja*, you're in for a tough few weeks of adjustment," warned Anna. "You have enough supplies—diapers and formula—for today, and you're likely to have a rough night tonight. But I'll put together a list, and you can go into town to shop for cloth diapers, changes of clothing, formula, that kind of thing."

"*Ja, danke!*" exclaimed Olivia. "That would be a huge help!"

"And I'll introduce you to my daughter Eva after church on Sunday," continued Anna. She winked. "I have a feeling you could use a friend, and Eva is about your age, though much more experienced with *bopplin*." She chuckled.

Olivia's heart warmed toward the older woman. She *could* use a friend, and she already put Anna in that category.

She walked back to her cottage with Helen tucked into the borrowed sling, feeling much more optimistic about the earth-shattering reality of becoming a mother to her niece.

"You said the seller had a family emergency back east?" remarked Andrew to Eli Miller as they rode in Eli's buggy. He knew Eli was acting as a casual real-estate agent, showing the property to interested parties. "And that's why they're selling?"

"Ja." Eli directed the horse down a side lane among dense conifers. "Apparently, their son-in-law passed away unexpectedly, leaving their daughter to cope with three tiny children, and she's expecting a *boppli* too. She needed help with the children as well as running their farm. The sellers needed to leave right away, so they boarded their livestock with neighbors and left. Those neighbors have been watering the garden and caring for the chickens. It's literally a turnkey farm, including cows and horses, for the buyer."

"What's the asking price?"

Eli named the sum, and Andrew winced and mentally dismissed the possibility of buying it. The property was almost twice as much as he was prepared to spend on a farm. He didn't doubt the land was worth it, but he just didn't have that kind of money on hand.

Besides, he wasn't in a hurry. This was just the first of what he assumed would be many properties he would review before deciding on which farm to buy. Such a decision couldn't be rushed, since farms among the Amish were usually lifelong endeavors.

However, he didn't say anything out loud to Eli. The older man was doing him a favor, and it would be rude to...

The trees parted, some buildings came into view and Andrew's whole world changed. He almost gasped.

A graceful log cabin with front and back porches had wreaths of Virginia creeper twining the posts and explosions of flowers around the home. Several outbuildings, including what looked like a small studio shed as well as an obvious chicken coop, were nearby. A large barn stood with its doors gaping open. An enormous raised-bed garden, fenced high against deer, was in the back of the house. The yard was fenced, with a slightly overgrown lawn, and broad pastures lined with dense conifers surrounded the buildings.

Andrew felt a chill down the back of his neck. This was it. This was the farm *Gott* wanted him to have. He had never been so sure of anything in his life—certainly more sure than he ever felt about courting Sarah.

"It's beautiful," he whispered.

Eli heard him. "*Ja*, the Schrocks were *gut* stewards of the land. The house is new, though it looks like it's been here for generations. We have a man here on the settlement who specializes in log homes, and he built this place about five years ago. The property comes with fifty acres. About ten is in woods, the rest is in pasture. They've been growing wheat for grain, as well as raising a few beef and dairy cattle. The garden is a bit over a quarter-acre in size, and there's a fairly new orchard over there." He pointed.

Andrew gulped. "I see why it's priced the way it is."

"It's actually not a bad price, considering everything that comes with it and the condition it's in," Eli agreed. "Let's go inside. I have the key since I just showed the property yesterday." He pulled the horse to a stop.

Andrew glanced sharply at the older man. Eli had shown the property to someone else just yesterday? A sense of urgency rose. How could he outbid another prospective buyer if he didn't even have enough money of his own to pay the asking price?

The situation seemed hopeless—futile—but he was desperate to look around and see if this farm was truly everything it seemed. He climbed down from the buggy and trailed in Eli's wake as they approached the empty cabin.

Three stately trees—two oaks and a maple—shadowed portions of the yard. They almost seemed out of place in this land of conifers, and Andrew knew their autumn foliage would be a touch of home when October came. The lawn was a bit shaggy—not unexpected, if neighbors were conducting distant upkeep.

The front porch still had a pair of rockers on it, looking cozy and inviting. "Does furniture come with the house?" asked Andrew in bewilderment.

"*Ja.* The Schrocks, they shipped some family heirlooms back with them, but they left behind things they didn't want to bother with. They were in a big hurry." He fitted the key in the lock and opened the paneled door.

Andrew stepped inside and saw…absolute perfection. Beams of sunlight shone through southern windows and illuminated golden hardwood floors, plain walls painted a cheerful cream, and a sturdy wood cookstove that straddled the kitchen and dining area. A solid-oak kitchen table was flanked by six chairs. Several comfortable padded chairs dotted the living room. Even the bedrooms had beds and dressers already in place—empty and stripped of linens, but useful nonetheless.

He followed Eli into the bedrooms, the bathroom, a large lean-to extension on the north side of the house, then through a back door to another wide porch overlooking the fenced garden. Everything was in exquisite order and looked like it had been cleaned to within an inch of its life the day before.

"How could they give this up?" he asked rhetorically as he and Eli stood on the back porch, looking across the garden beds.

Eli glanced at him. "Family is more important," he said simply.

Andrew gulped. "*Ja*, of course. But this looks like a bit of paradise on earth."

"It's certainly one of the prettier farms around here," the older man agreed. "*Komm*, I'll show you the rest."

No matter how closely Andrew peered into corners and stalls and pastures, he could find nothing wrong with the property. The garden was exquisite, with tidy raised beds watered by a drip-irrigation system. The chickens were fed and watered, their coop was clean and there were even some ungathered eggs in a couple of the nest boxes. The empty barn had spacious stalls for both horses and cows, fenced feed lots, feeding boxes, calf pens and a milking stall. There was even a buggy and a wagon parked inside.

Eli led him on a brief wider tour of the outlying portions of the property. Andrew noted the strong fencing, the subdivided pastures, the woodlot where select trees were cut for winter firewood. The woodshed was even stacked high with dried and split firewood to last through the upcoming winter. Everything, it seemed, was ready for him to take possession and sink into the happy farm life he wanted for himself. Everything, that is, except the cost.

He couldn't argue that the asking price wasn't fair. But it far exceeded the amount of money he had saved up.

When the tour ended after two hours of careful inspection, Eli paused and leaned against the split-rail fence encircling the broad yard. "What do you think?" he asked.

Andrew scrubbed a hand across his face. "I think I want this place so badly I can almost taste it," he admitted.

"I can understand that. It's a beautiful spot. Well, I'm sure the Schrocks will be delighted to have someone committed to buying it…"

"But I don't have enough money," Andrew blurted out.

Eli's brow furrowed. "Oh. That's a problem, then. Well, I know of a couple other places I could show you. They're not as nice as this, but—"

"Nein." Andrew shook his head. "I want this place. Let me think. There must be some way…"

"I wouldn't delay too long, young man. The family I showed it to yesterday was quite interested as well, but they have to arrange financing."

Andrew looked over at the house. Already he was mentally putting down roots. He could see himself sitting on one of those porch rockers, perhaps with a dog at his feet. He could see the barn stocked with a couple of plow horses and a buggy horse. Two Jersey cows for milk, a feeder calf for beef, maybe a pig or two. The garden was producing strawberries, and he saw tiny fruit growing on the peach, apple and pear trees.

This farm was meant for him. He was certain of it. There *had* to be a way to pay for it. But how?

Could he get a loan from a bank? Eli had already warned that while lenders in Amish states back east have had generations to get used to Amish finances, the banks in Pierce weren't quite sure how to handle the unorthodox considerations of the church, though they were gradually coming around. Up until this point, Andrew hadn't considered the issue, since he'd always assumed any property he bought would be paid for by him, and him alone...

Eli Miller was quiet during this silent debate. Finally, the older man made a gesture. "Are you ready to go back?"

"Ja." Andrew gave a long, lingering look back at the house, then climbed into the buggy seat. His brain flip-flopped first one way, then another. How could he get the money to buy this farm? He had no collateral, nothing he could offer a bank to lend him the funds.

As if aware of the mental turmoil churning in his brain, Eli stayed quiet on the ride back to the Miller farm. It wasn't until they pulled up to the house that the older man looked at him. "Will you be *oll recht*?"

"Ja." Andrew pinched the brim of his nose and silently said a prayer. "Just have a lot of thinking to do, that's all. *Vielen dank* for showing me the farm, Eli."

"Bitte."

Andrew strode toward the bunkhouse. The interior was sparse and somehow sterile. His roommates were gone. Andrew sat down on the edge of the bed, dropped his head in his hands and wondered what to do.

Suddenly, an idea rocketed through his brain so powerfully that he sprang to his feet and stood frozen, thinking. Could he…?

It was a crazy idea, but perhaps *Gott* had sent the solution to his problem. There was only one way to find out.

Galvanized, he snatched up his hat and strode out of the bunkhouse into the low evening sunshine. It was a half-mile walk, and he covered the distance with determined steps.

The front door to Olivia's cabin was closed, but the windows were open, inviting in the sweet evening air. Andrew knocked on her door, knowing he must look wild and unhinged.

She opened the door cautiously and looked startled to see him. Before she could even open her mouth for a greeting, he blurted out, "How would you like to buy a farm with me?"

Chapter Four

Olivia had had a difficult day of coping with her new life as a mom. She was in no mood for jokes, and surely that's why Andrew was here. Who asked that kind of question of someone he had only met that morning?

"Nein," she replied shortly, and started to close the door.

He stopped her. "Wait, Olivia. I'm serious. Eli Miller showed me a farm this afternoon that's the closest thing I've seen to paradise on earth, but I can't afford it. If we join our finances, we can buy it..."

"Andrew, I don't even know you," she replied crossly. "I've had a long, hard day trying to deal with my niece, and suddenly you show up on my doorstep and want me to give you all the money I got from the sale of *Daed's* farm? *Nein.*" Once again, she tried to close the door.

But the man was persistent. "Listen to me," he said, urgency in his voice. "Someone else is interested in this property, but I can't let them have it. This farm is everything I've ever wanted. Since you were interested in buying a place of your own, too, we could both have it!"

"I was interested in a place of my own, *ja*, but that's the important part. *Of my own.* Not with you, not with anyone else. Except little Helen now."

"But that's just it," he replied in a persuasive voice. "If you join with me to help buy this farm, there's plenty of room to raise Helen. And…and I could stand in as a father for her."

The man was mad. Olivia passed a weary hand over her face. "Look, Andrew, I just got the baby to sleep, and I'm tired myself. Can we talk about this tomorrow?"

"Will you come look at the farm with me tomorrow? You might change your mind once you see it."

"*Ja*, sure. Fine. Whatever." Anything to get rid of the man. *"Gude nacht."* This time she succeeded in closing the door.

She glanced through the door to her bedroom, but little Helen still slept. After her crash course in mothering that afternoon, she had managed to get the hang of the sling, but caring for a baby was, she swiftly realized, going to be a full-time job. She was starting to seriously doubt whether she should follow through on that impulsive decision to raise her father's only grandchild, or give up and hand the baby over to someone more qualified.

And now here was the local handyman showing up on her doorstep, bleating about joining finances to buy something *he* wanted. Crazy talk.

She sighed, and her confidence ebbed even lower. She had basket orders to fill. She also wanted to experiment with some of the natural materials found around her here in Montana. Taking care of a *boppli*, she now knew, would put a crimp in her work schedule.

Nor did she have much room. The rental cabin was already crammed with her basket-making materials, and at present it was utterly unsafe for a baby. While she had no personal experience caring for children, everyone around her in Pennsylvania did. She had watched, with admiration, the tag-team efforts of the couples, with both parents pitching in.

Besides, most Amish mothers didn't work when their children were young. Usually, it was just the young, unmarried girls who worked, or older women whose children were grown. In thinking she could raise Helen, was she setting herself up for failure—of either her business or of her mothering—by taking on the task of being a single mom? With piercing clarity, she suddenly understood why her father had lost control of Adele, since he was working as well as raising his daughters as a single dad.

She felt a moment of panic as she glanced at the baby slumbering in the basket in her bedroom. Would Adele's baby turn out to be like... Adele?

She sat back down at the kitchen table and continued the project Andrew's visit had interrupted, which was weaving a basket of intricate design she hoped to sell in town. She had a generous nest egg from the sale of her *daed's* house, true, but she didn't want to dip into it for day-to-day living expenses. For that, she had her basketry skills.

But Andrew's strange visit made her think about what she wanted for her future. She hadn't really visualized anything beyond a vague desire for a workroom of her own and a spot for a nice garden. And maybe some chickens. This could be accomplished on a small half-acre plot. Not that she would mind more room for a few cows, but it wasn't essential. She wasn't farming for a family. She was just supporting herself.

While she was grateful for Andrew's help today with Helen, she had to admit he had just posed the oddest question she had ever received. Go halves on a farm she'd never seen, with a man she'd just met? No possible way.

At a moment when she was involved in a particularly critical knot on the basket, Olivia heard Helen stir and begin crying. A quick glance at the clock in the kitchen revealed the baby had only been sleeping less than an hour. She grimaced. She had a feeling she was in for a long night. With a martyred sigh, she finished her knot and got up to tend to the infant.

Her predictions came to pass. Olivia changed Helen. She fed her. She rocked her. She walked with her, pacing up and down through a cleared pathway in the room among the organic debris used for basketry. At intervals she laid the baby in the makeshift cradle and tried to snatch some sleep herself. Yet despite her fatigue, there was a seed of love for the infant beginning to germinate. This was her niece, her father's only grandchild, the daughter of her sister.

When dawn broke through the pine trees shading the house, Olivia splashed cold water on her face, gazed down at the (finally!) sleeping baby and came to a grim conclusion: if she was going to keep Helen, she wouldn't be able to do it alone.

What had Andrew said? *If you join with me to help buy this farm, there's plenty of room to raise Helen. And...and I could stand in as a father for her.*

Did he mean it, or was it just a desperate offer in a desperate attempt to get to her money?

In her sleep-deprived state, Olivia almost

didn't care. He'd shown himself to be competent with the baby, far more competent than herself. He was gentle with the infant. He seemed like a kind man. If his offer to co-parent Helen came at the cost of her own privacy in co-owning this farm, then maybe—just maybe—it was worth considering.

She made herself a cup of tea and sank down into the rocking chair she had so recently vacated. She placed the cup on the small table nearby, then rocked and thought about Andrew's words...

A knock on the door made her jump awake. She'd fallen asleep in the rocking chair for two hours! Knuckling sleep from her eyes, she stumbled for the door, tightening the tie on her bathrobe. She pulled open the door to see Andrew, looking infuriatingly well rested, with a toolbox in hand.

"Guder mariye." He eyed her with some sympathy. "Bad night?"

"*Ja.* Barely slept." She yawned. "I'm sorry..."

"Don't be. I would have been surprised if you'd gotten a *good* night's sleep."

She gestured toward his toolbox. "Are you here to do more repairs?"

"*Ja*, but not on the roof this time. And I'm also delivering a message. Anna Miller sent a detailed list of what you might want to get for the *boppli* and where to get it." He dug into his pocket and handed over a piece of paper.

"*Ja, gut.*" She took the list and glanced over it. It was, indeed, very detailed. "I could go tomorrow, then. Andrew…" She trailed off. In her fatigued state, perhaps this wasn't the best time to bring up last night's conversation. Abruptly, she decided to press on. "Last night you said something in passing. I wonder if you were serious."

An expression of hope crossed his face. "You mean about co-funding the farm?"

"*Ja*, but something more. You said if I pitched in to buy it, you could stand in as a father for Helen. Were you serious?"

He hesitated. "*Ja.* If that's what it takes to get you to agree, then of course."

She wasn't sure she liked his mercenary logic, but she was too tired—and increasingly desperate—to argue. "Then we might be able to come to some sort of agreement."

A look of wild happiness drenched his face, and his smile rivaled the sun. "*Danke*, Olivia!" For a moment he looked as though he might spontaneously embrace her in his enthusiasm, but he didn't. "This is the prettiest farm I've ever seen! I'll borrow Eli's rig, and we can go look at it this afternoon, if you like!"

She couldn't help but smile at his eagerness.

"*Ja, gut.* Meanwhile..." She cocked an ear. "It sounds like Helen is awake."

"Do you want me to jump in now and take care of her? You might be able to snatch a nap."

The idea was tempting, but she shook her head. "You have work to do for the Millers. This is a business arrangement, Andrew, and it will take time to work out the details."

"But you won't regret it, Olivia, I promise. I'll do my best to become little Helen's *daed* and make your burden easier."

She nodded and smiled. "I reserve the right to back out if the farm isn't what you say it is. I have no intention of wasting my money on a bad investment. But we might be able to work things out. Now, I must go and take care of the baby." *And get dressed*, she added silently.

She closed the door on the still-grinning Andrew and went to tend to Helen. A trickle of worry went through her. What had she agreed to in her sleep-deprived state? Was she doing something foolish? Was she wasting her money? She barely even knew the man!

She lifted the fussing baby from the padded basket and went to change her diaper, gnawing at the concerns about Andrew like a dog gnaws on a bone. One thing was certain: this would be nothing more than a business arrangement. She intended to have a contract drawn up by an attorney making that perfectly clear.

She sat down in the rocking chair and slipped the tip of the bottle into Helen's mouth. The infant immediately began drinking, her dark eyes focused on Olivia's face with peculiar intensity.

She was tired, yes…but the faint stirrings of love for the baby that were almost extinguished by her sleepless night came back, stronger this time. Helen *did* resemble Adele. Olivia made a silent promise to cultivate the best part of the baby's personality and discourage the rebellion that had turned Adele away from her family and her faith. And, despite her doubts about contracting with Andrew or funding his dream, it was encouraging to think she might not be facing the daunting task of raising a child on her own.

It wasn't until later that a thought occurred to her: What *was* the farm even like? Was it as picturesque as Andrew implied? What if she hated it?

She might have made a verbal agreement, but she felt no obligation to follow through and part with her money if the property didn't interest her.

A farm! And not just any farm—the farm of his dreams! It was all Andrew could do to not pump a fist in the air. He had been right—*Gott* had given him the idea to propose this arrangement to Olivia. And if the cost of buying his dream property was to help out with the *boppli*... Well, he liked children, and little Helen was darling. He didn't see that as an impediment to his goals.

He went about his repair tasks with a smile on his face, whistling a cheerful tune. The world seemed bathed in a golden glow. He took pleasure in his work, especially since he would soon be applying his skills to his very own place. Well, his and Olivia's very own place.

He was impatient for the day to pass until Olivia was ready to go see the property. He was eager to view it again as well, to see if it was as perfect as he remembered or if he was embroidering a fantasy in his mind.

After two hours, his miscellaneous tasks were done. Should he knock on the door and let her know he was leaving, and to arrange the right time to pick her up in the buggy? He didn't know if the baby—or Olivia—was sleeping. He compromised by knocking softly.

She answered promptly, clutching a handful of cattail leaves and looking distracted, as if caught in the middle of a task.

"I'm finished with my repair work," he told her. "Are you still interested in seeing the farm this afternoon?"

"*Ja*, sure." She waved the cattail leaves. "I'm trying to finish up a basket, but I can stop whenever you want to go. What time did you have in mind?"

"How about one o'clock-ish, after lunch? I can bring the buggy by so you don't have to walk over with Helen."

"*Gut.*" She nodded. "I'll be ready."

"*Danke*, Olivia," he said seriously. "This means a lot to me."

She gave him a thin smile. "Remember, I reserve the right to say no if I don't like the property."

"I can't see how you *couldn't* like it, but I understand." He touched the brim of his hat. "See you at one."

He walked back toward the Millers' place, toolbox in hand. He dropped his things in the bunkhouse and went to find Eli.

"*Ja*, sure, you can borrow the buggy," said the older man. "But I thought you didn't have enough money to purchase the farm?"

Andrew wasn't sure he wanted to delve into the intricacies of his unorthodox financing arrangement until things were a little more decided. "I might have come up with a way," he prevaricated, "but I don't want to discuss it until I'm sure."

Eli didn't press. Instead, he handed over the

farm's house key and told Andrew to lock up when he was finished looking the place over.

Andrew went back to the bunkhouse and made himself a frugal lunch while impatiently watching the clock. Was he moving too fast? Would he regret teaming up with Olivia solely to buy the property? He tried to pray about it, but he was too restless. His chaotic thoughts wouldn't settle.

Finally, it was time to hitch up the horse and pick up Olivia. He was gratified to see her emerge from her cabin, the baby tucked in the borrowed sling, clutching a basket of feeding and diaper supplies.

"Shall I take the baby?" he offered.

"I'm not sure yet." She handed him the basket and hitched up her skirts. "I'm still getting used to carrying her in the sling—carrying her at all, for that matter—so let's see if I can manage."

She did manage, but only after one or two false starts that had the baby awake and Olivia laughing. He was pleased to see her good humor through what was still, after all, a trying time for her.

When she was comfortably seated and the baby secure, Andrew clucked to the horse and started down the road. "I was worried you might change your mind," he confessed.

"I haven't made *up* my mind," she retorted,

though without rancor. "Since I haven't seen the property yet. But I'll admit the thought of having some help with the baby is what compelled me to tentatively agree."

"And I can promise you I'll follow through," he replied. "I don't break my promises."

She looked around as he guided the horse deeper into the Amish settlement where cars were seldom seen. He waved to one or two people walking, still not sure of everyone's names.

"It *is* pretty," she admitted as they passed under fir trees that dappled the sunlight. "Very different from Pennsylvania, but I like it."

"Wait until you see the farm," he said eagerly. He told her what Eli had related about the family emergency that was forcing the owners to sell. "I hate the thought of benefitting from their misfortune, but I'll admit, this place will make your jaw drop."

"I don't think I've ever seen anyone as eager as you over a piece of land," she said. "You said livestock comes with it?"

"*Ja*. There are chickens still in their coop, and it has a full garden. The cows and horses are being boarded by the same people who come in every day to check on the chickens and to keep the garden watered. There's even a buggy and a wagon in the barn. They come with the house."

"A garden would be nice." Olivia looked down

at the baby slung across her chest. "I miss my old garden. I'd cultivated it for years."

"This is all raised beds, with drip irrigation. It looks like it's doing well—though, of course, the sellers may not have planted it up with everything you might prefer."

"I wonder if it has a place I can set up my basket-making supplies," she mused. "Especially if I'm keeping Helen, I'll need to keep dangerous things out of her reach once she's old enough to crawl."

"It has a sort of lean-to room," he offered. "It's fairly good-sized. You can look it over and see if it would work for you."

Olivia suddenly chuckled. He angled her a look. "What's so funny?"

"Does it seem like *Gott* is pushing us toward this place, if it has everything either of us ever wanted in a farm?"

"Ja!" he exclaimed, pleased she understood. "That's why I'm hoping you'll be as delighted with it as I am. A working farm, already established, means I can bring in income right away rather than waiting for things to *become* established. Since I'll be using up just about every last cent I have saved up to buy it, that gives me some comfort. I won't have much of a financial cushion once I—we—buy the place."

"Neither will I," she warned. "That's why I

can't give a definite *ja* until I see it. How much further?"

"Maybe half a mile." He was stabbed by sudden doubt. "I pray you'll find the property just as wonderful as I do."

"And if I don't?" She looked over at him. "Seriously, Andrew, is it like you to get so worked up over something that you would make such an unconventional proposal?"

"Nein," he replied. "I've never felt like this before about anything, including the farm I grew up on. It—it just *speaks* to me. I can't help but feel *Gott* wants me there."

"Or maybe that's your excuse. I'm sorry to say this, but at the moment, it sounds like you're afflicted with a serious case of coveting."

He startled. "Am I?" He considered his chaotic emotions. "You may be right," he said slowly. "I've never felt this way before. I can see why *Gott* warns us about such things." Should he give up on the whole concept of buying the farm? The very thought pained him.

"Well, if it works out, we'll both benefit." Olivia looked down at the baby in the sling, and he saw affection on her face. "I tried to get some work done today, and it was almost impossible. I have orders to fill, and yet I could barely get anything done."

"Then we can work out a schedule. If I'm

working a farm, my time is flexible. You'll see, Olivia. We'll work it out. Look…" He pointed. "We turn up there. The first part of the driveway is kind of hidden in trees, then everything opens up."

He directed the horse onto the narrow driveway. For a moment he closed his eyes and breathed a formless prayer that she would find the property as enchanting as he did.

She was quiet as the horse walked the hundred yards or so of dark conifers, almost a tunnel of needles, with a bright circle of light ahead of them where the trees ended and the land opened up.

With an instinctive sense of drama, Andrew slowed the horse a bit more, delaying for a few seconds the theatrical moment when the house would come into view through the tunnel of trees. He realized his heart was thudding as if he'd been working hard, though he recognized it was from nervous anticipation. What if she didn't want to go in with him on the purchase? He could hardly bear the thought. "Coveting," he muttered to himself through gritted teeth.

The inevitable moment came when the horse and buggy emerged from the tunnel of trees. He heard a gasp, and pulled the horse to a stop.

He glanced over at Olivia. She sat stock-still, staring, her mouth agape.

Chapter Five

Olivia stared at the scene before her, unable to believe her eyes. It was as if a storybook farm had come to life and was presented before them.

The horse walked forward at a sedate pace as she drank in the sight of the beautifully proportioned log home with its generous front and back porches, wreaths of Virginia creeper, the lawn enclosed by split-rail fencing reinforced with wire, the profusion of colorful flowers lining the porches and sprouting from hanging baskets. The crow of a rooster punctuated the chatter of birdsong.

It took a few moments for her to tear her eyes off the house to notice the barn, outbuildings and garden.

"Magnificent," she breathed.

"*Ja*, I thought so too," Andrew said beside her. She heard a note of relief in his voice. "In fact, I'm glad to see it again today. I wasn't sure if I was just embellishing a fantasy in my mind or if it was actually as beautiful as I remember."

He directed the horse toward a fir tree overshadowing a hitching post. After climbing down from the buggy, he came around to give Olivia his hand while she clutched the baby to her chest. Olivia seldom had men help her out of buggies, and tried not to read anything into the courteous gesture.

Little Helen woke up and made some noises of protest but settled back down when Olivia patted her back and crooned to her. The baby seemed content to be snug in the sling and moving, and Olivia remembered what Anna had told her about that notion.

They walked up the steps to the front porch, where the rockers beckoned invitingly. "What a view, *nein*?" she asked rhetorically, gesturing through the Virginia creeper toward the broad green lawn and protective cluster of trees blocking the view of the road.

"*Ja.*" Andrew looked upward at the underside of the porch roof as if assessing its strength. "Eli said this place was only built five years ago, but it has an air of permanence I find appealing."

"Let's go in." She heard the eagerness in her own voice and had a feeling her financial future was sealed.

Olivia had been in very few log cabins in her life, and those she had seen hadn't appealed to her, with their vaulted ceilings and faux-rustic air that cloaked every possible modern convenience. But this cabin wasn't like that. Though fairly new, it was built for an Amish family, and so highlighted the Plain features and layout she preferred.

There wasn't anything inside the home that didn't charm her, from the heavy wood cookstove to the spacious living room. Through south-facing windows, beams of sunlight highlighted honey-colored wood floors. She glanced over some of the furniture pieces left behind by the sellers and mentally meshed it with the few pieces she herself had brought from Pennsylvania.

To his credit, Andrew didn't say much as she poked into corners and explored the house. He didn't badger or coerce. He simply let the house speak for itself, and it had a powerful voice.

It also worked. As Andrew mentioned, it was as if *Gott* had sent her the perfect place to live. With Helen sleeping snugly in the sling, she and Andrew paced around every foot of the house and property. She saw the lean-to that would, as he'd predicted, make an ideal studio for her basketry. They viewed the garden, the orchard, the wheat field, the pastures, the chicken coop, the barn. Even having a buggy and wagon come with the property was a thrill.

All this could be hers…with one codicil: she

would have to join forces with Andrew. He was still a stranger, and she couldn't help but worry it might not work out if they were incompatible.

"See, the stalls are all ready for livestock," Andrew pointed out with enthusiasm. "I can bring the animals back from where they're being boarded and get into dairy production right away. That will help earn money."

"And don't forget the garden. Yoder's store in town will sell produce," she reminded him. "And the chickens. Eggs always sell."

But there was more. As they neared the end of their leisurely exploration, for the first time, she realized what this business arrangement meant: that essentially she and Andrew would be cohabitating, partners in work but not in life. As a plain spinster approaching her thirtieth birthday, it was more than Olivia ever anticipated. What would it be like, living with a man? She supposed she would soon find out.

But now, having seen the property, she understood far better why Andrew was willing to promise so much to buy the farm. Originally, she had thought to spend her nest egg money on a small place just suitable for her own needs. But there was something about this property that called to her, that created a yearning she couldn't shake. Was this coveting? If so, it was a far more powerful emotion than she'd ever realized.

As they approached the house one last time, Helen woke up and began fussing. "I'll need to change and feed her," she told him. "I can do it on the porch."

"*Ja, gut.* I'll get the basket of supplies from the buggy."

She watched him as he trotted over to the conveyance. The fact that he'd offered to fetch the needed items without thought and without complaint was a promising sign. He seemed like a *gut* man. But was he a man she could partner with for the sole purpose of co-owning this beautiful piece of land? Could she partner with him to raise Helen?

And a thin little element of despair flared up. He was catering to her and Helen for an ulterior purpose: to obtain the farm. Not for her, personally. It was a bitter pill Olivia had swallowed years ago, but every so often the bad taste cropped up and unsettled her.

After attending to Helen's hygiene needs, Olivia settled in one of the rocking chairs on the porch and started to feed the baby. She rocked and looked at the view and, like Andrew, coveted this for her very own.

"I want in," she told him quietly.

His smile was ecstatic as he took the other rocking chair. "Then, with *Gott's* help, we'll make this work," he told her.

"Andrew..." She trailed off for a moment, then decided to be honest. "I know this will be a business arrangement, and I insist that we get paperwork drawn up by an attorney before committing my money to buy this place. But there's more to it than that. For all intents and purposes, we'll...we'll be living together." She felt herself blush. "I've never been courted. I don't know how we'll get around the natural intimacy that being housemates will make us."

"Ja." He frowned and rubbed his chin thoughtfully. "In fact, you bring up something I hadn't considered in all my giddiness about this farm. It's no light thing to have an unmarried couple residing in the same home. The fact is, we may not be able to both live here without risking *meidung*. Shunning. No piece of property is worth that."

"I agree. I would never jeopardize my standing in the church just because I fell in love with a farm."

"Then maybe we'd better go talk to the bishop first and lay everything before him. He'll have the final say about whether such an arrangement will be permitted."

"He may say *nein*."

"Ja, he may." He stared out at the lawn. "In which case, we should be prepared to offer alternatives. For example, we could reside in separate

residences on the property." He gestured. "That shed over there could be outfitted for a sort of bunkhouse. That's one possibility."

"*Ja*. Another possibility is we co-own the property, but one of us resides elsewhere—in town or something. Or I stay in my cottage. Or you stay in the bunkhouse. In other words, one of us lives off the property."

"I hope it doesn't come to that," Andrew remarked. "The whole purpose is to live here and enjoy its amenities."

Olivia gave him a half smile and shook her head. "Things are moving so fast. A baby. A farm. A partner. It's *seltsam*. Weird."

He hesitated. "From the moment I set eyes on this place, I convinced myself it's where *Gott* wanted me to be. I'm trying to discern if it's not just a bad case of coveting, as you said earlier. But having seen it, I would do almost anything to buy it."

"Including partnering with the plainest woman on the settlement?" There, she'd said it.

Andrew looked startled. "You, plain?" he blurted out. "That hadn't occurred to me."

Was he being truthful? It was hard to say. He'd just finished stating he would do anything to buy this farm…including, possibly, fibbing about her looks.

Well, in the end it didn't matter if he thought

she was plain or not. It was just a business arrangement. Nothing more, nothing less. She wanted this property just as badly as he did... though, she had to admit he was a lot easier on the eyes than she was.

Helen gave a tiny grunt and fell off the bottle. Olivia hitched the infant over her shoulder and patted the little back until she heard a delicate *braaap*. She stood up and fitted the sling around the baby.

But Andrew remained in the rocking chair, staring out at the lawn with vacant eyes as if deep in thought. "It won't work," he finally muttered.

"What won't work?"

"The more I think about it, the more I believe the bishop won't permit this kind of arrangement."

She sank back into the rocking chair. It was a distressing thought, but she knew he was right. "*Ja*, I agree," she said. "I can't imagine he'll allow this. It sets a dangerous precedent to the church. Oh, Andrew, what are we going to do?"

Andrew gazed around at the property. Despair clutched at his heart. "I don't know," he admitted. "All I can see is growing old here, rocking on this porch and enjoying the view. This farm has the potential for everything I've ever wanted to do. Having found it, I can't bear the thought of losing it."

"I understand the feeling." She sighed. "Yesterday I was ready to accuse you of coveting, yet today it seems I'm afflicted with the same sin. I want this place just as badly."

A thought occurred to him. It was just as wild a thought that had sent him to her doorstep to see if she wanted to buy a farm in the first place. Was the idea sent by *Gott*? "There's one possible solution..." He knew his voice sounded odd.

She glanced at him sharply. "And what is that?"

He stayed silent a moment, then turned to face her. "We could get married."

He saw utter shock on her face. For a few heartbeats, there was silence except for birdsong. The rooster crowed in the distance. Somewhere far off, he heard a dog bark. He saw her arms reflexively clutch Helen a little tighter in the sling.

Finally, she spoke, and her voice was grim. "Andrew, marriage is forever. Do you really want to be yoked with a woman like me?"

Whatever reaction he might have expected, it wasn't this. He was genuinely bewildered. "A woman like you? What do you mean?"

Despair crossed her face. "Handsome men don't marry plain women."

While he was pleased to be called handsome, he wondered at her self-deprecation. "That's the second time you've said that. It bothers me."

"Well, it bothers me too." She looked severe. "You would regret marrying me, Andrew. Trust me."

Did she really think she was the plainest woman on the settlement? Did that really mean so much to her? He slowed his chaotic thoughts down and tried to imagine things from her perspective: unmarried, unlikely to *get* married, compelled to earn a living as a single woman. Did she long to change that? He didn't know. Unexpectedly, he felt a trace of humor go through him. Maybe he could convince her. "I never told you about my courtship back in Ohio, did I?"

"Courtship?" Wariness crossed her face.

"*Ja.* Did it occur to you to ask why I'm not married?"

She replied cautiously, "I did wonder, *ja.* But I also figured it was none of my business."

"Well, it's no secret." He settled back in the rocker. "Here's what happened. I was courting the prettiest girl in our church. And when I say *pretty*, that was an understatement. She was beautiful, meltingly beautiful. I was bedazzled, absolutely besotted. Everywhere she went, people stared at her, and she loved it. I could hardly believe that someone as gorgeous as Sarah would allow a clod like me to court her. And in the end, I was right."

She winced. "What happened?"

"It was very simple. She found someone else she preferred more and dumped me."

Olivia sucked in her breath but said nothing.

He nodded. "It's like she hardly considered the shattered pieces she left in her wake. She took away all my dreams. All my plans. My future family with *kinner*. I had been saving aggressively for a farm so I'd have the means to support her and a family, and that motivation was taken away too. In that moment, it was like blinders were stripped from my eyes, and I recognized how little her beauty meant. What good is beauty if the heart doesn't match the face?"

She nodded. "I understand that far more than I should."

"Perhaps you do, if your sister is as beautiful as you claim. Well, needless to say, it changed me. I stayed in my hometown and worked like crazy to save money for my own farm, only this time I knew it wasn't for anyone else but me. Not for Sarah, not for the family I knew I'd never have with her. When I'd saved enough, I left and came here to Montana." He pinched the bridge of his nose and closed his eyes for a moment. "But, having been burned badly by a beautiful woman, it left me soured on beautiful women. Beauty doesn't impress me. In fact, I'm suspicious of it. I decided it was better to stay single than to risk involvement with another shallow woman. I decided a farm would take the place of the family Sarah snatched from my grasp. Now, having found the farm, I don't want to let it go." He concluded by saying, "A pretty face means very little to me now, Olivia. I've learned strength of character is far more important. Can you deny you possess that in abundance?"

She was silent a moment. After a bit she spoke, and her voice held bitterness. "Having grown up in the shadow of a beautiful sister, I understand a lot of what you went through. Adele caused my father no end of heartache as she made bad choice after bad choice, much of it based on the fact that she knew she was beautiful and would be more likely to get away with it. I pray her daughter doesn't follow in her wake." She hugged the baby to her.

"So we're both single, in a way, because of beauty."

"*Ja*, I suppose. Or the lack of it, in my case." She shrugged. "Long ago, I set myself to being single, and my goal was to buy a small place and support myself with my basketry. Two things have changed that. One, having Helen dumped on my doorstep means my situation is altered. And two, seeing this farm…well, I have to agree with you, it's stunning beyond belief." She paused. "So yes, Andrew, I will marry you. A marriage of convenience *only*," she added.

Relief flooded him and he smiled broadly. Suddenly, the world seemed rosy again. "*Danke*, Olivia! This gives us both a fighting chance to follow through with the purchase. We can still have the paperwork drawn up that gives us, legally, half shares on the property. But getting married will give us legitimacy in the eyes of the church."

"Whew." She slumped into the rocking chair and gave him a small grin. "What are we getting ourselves into, Andrew?"

He grinned back, liking the spark of risk-taking in her. "An adventure, but one you won't regret. I will work hard, Olivia, and I *will* be a father to Helen. While you and I may see this as merely a contractual agreement, Helen will never suffer from it. People have started out their married lives under worse circumstances and made it work."

"Now we have to convince the bishop our desire to get married is legitimate," she warned. "He may still deny us."

"*Ja*, he may." Concern furrowed his brow. "But he can't stop us from buying the place, though we may have to resort to a purely contractual agreement if that's the case. If you're still willing to commit your money, that is."

"To own this farm? Absolutely." She gazed out at the yard, and he could almost see her mentally putting down the same roots he himself felt. "And since I have no other prospects, or likelihood of prospects, I'm even willing to engage in a marriage of convenience since I'll benefit from it quite a bit. Possibly more than you."

She was brave, he realized. Marriage was what most young women dreamed of their whole lives, and to have her admit she was willing to form a purely contractual relationship with him spoke of her certainty that nothing better would ever come along. No wonder she had cultivated her basket-making skills to such a high level; it was an ideal means to support herself.

"You said you planned to support yourself with your baskets," he said. "Does it really bring in enough money to do that?"

"Ja." She spoke with confidence. "I've built up quite a *gut* wholesale market and ship baskets all over the country. One thing I haven't done yet is stop at Yoder's Mercantile in town and see if they're willing to sell some for me."

"Then once we get established here, we'll set up regular hours for when you need to work, and that's when I'll take care of the *boppli*."

"Danke, Andrew." Her voice held gratitude. "Just having her for as short a time as I have makes me realize how hard it would be to keep up with my orders while caring for her. And you were right—that lean-to addition on the side of

the house will make an ideal studio for me." She pointed.

"I keep seeing the hand of *Gott* in all this," he mused. "This place is perfect for you. It's perfect for me. Together we have the ability to purchase the farm outright, which means no mortgage payments, which means we can live fairly cheaply. Together we have the ways to raise an unexpected baby. How else can we describe this except as *Gott's* will?"

"Well, let's not count our chickens before they hatch." She looked down at Helen, but the baby had fallen asleep. "We need to talk to the bishop first, since he's the biggest hurdle. When should we do that?"

"Are you up for right away?" He looked eager again. "It's Wednesday afternoon. He's probably home. I know it's a bit rude to drop in without an appointment, but if nothing else, we can ask to see him at a time when it's more convenient."

"*Ja*, now is as *gut* a time as any." A little awkwardly, since the baby was in the sling across her chest, she rose from the rocking chair. "*Komm*. We have much to tell the bishop, starting with how this little one was left on my doorstep."

"I agree." He rose and locked the door behind them and pocketed the key. "I'm willing to guess this will be the strangest request he's had in a long time."

Chapter Six

The bishop, Samuel Beiler, and his wife, Lois, lived in what looked like a made-over barn perched on a wide lawn amid the pines and firs, with a graceful porch in front. A large garden was adjacent to the lawn. Andrew directed the horse into their driveway and climbed down to tie the animal to a hitching post under a tree. Then he came around to assist Olivia from the buggy.

Olivia clutched Helen in the sling against her chest. "Might want to grab the diaper basket, just in case." She heard her own voice tremble a bit.

Andrew shot her a glance. "Nervous?"

"*Ja*, maybe. A lot hinges on this visit."

"He may not be home... *Nein*, there he is."

Olivia glanced over and saw the church leader, lanky and with a wispy gray beard, emerge from the house onto the porch. He smiled and waved a greeting.

"Courage," muttered Andrew as he accompanied her toward the house. Olivia wondered whether the word was for herself or for him.

"Andrew! And..." Bishop Beiler peered closer. "Olivia? This is a surprise."

"*Ja*, we have some things to discuss with you," replied Andrew. "Do you have time now, or can we make an appointment later?"

"Now is fine." He made a gesture of welcome, then peered more closely at Olivia. "Are you carrying...a *boppli*?"

"*Ja*." She gave the church leader what she hoped was a brave smile. "A lot has happened in the last day or two."

"Evidently. Well, *komm* in."

The Beilers' living room was a typical Plain space, with a braided rag rug and worn but comfortable furniture. Lois Beiler emerged from the kitchen, plump and smiling. "*Welkom!*" She did an almost comical double take upon seeing Olivia carrying an infant in the sling. "Is that a *boppli*?"

"*Ja*." Olivia gave Helen a gentle pat on the back.

"Is this matter private that you want to discuss, or can Lois be present?" asked the bishop.

"Having Lois here might be a huge help," replied Andrew. "A woman's perspective is just what we need."

"Let me go get some iced tea," murmured Lois, and disappeared back into the kitchen.

"Please, be seated." The bishop gestured toward some seats. "And tell me who this little one is."

"Her name is Helen," replied Olivia. "She's my niece and is one of the things we're here to discuss."

Lois reemerged with a tray of frosty glasses, which she handed around. "So where did this little one come from?" she asked.

Olivia sighed. "Literally, I found her on my doorstep. She's my older sister's baby. My sister has been a…a *challenge* since she was a youngie. She left the faith long ago, though she drops back into my life every so often to recharge, usually between relationships. This time she didn't even knock at the door. She just left the baby outside on the step with a suitcase and a note saying she's not cut out for motherhood, and she's on her way to Europe with a new man."

Both Bishop Beiler and Lois sucked in a shocked breath.

Olivia nodded. "I panicked. The baby was crying, and I had no idea what to do. Andrew happened to knock on the door at that moment, and I yanked him into the house and demanded help. To my surprise, he did." She shot Andrew a grin. "In fact, he knew exactly what to do."

"I have a lot of younger siblings," Andrew clarified.

"There's no question about keeping her," continued Olivia, sobering up. "Apparently, Helen—the *boppli*—was born on May first, the very day my *daed* died." She blinked back tears. "He always wanted grandchildren, and didn't live long enough to see any. Helen was also my mother's name. She died when I was two years old. I—I can't give Helen away. In other words, I feel strongly that *Gott* wants me to raise this baby."

"*Ja,* I can understand that," said Lois. Her eyes were suspiciously bright. "But it won't be easy for you, raising a baby on your own."

"*Ja,* I know—"

"That's where I come in," interrupted Andrew. "I'm proposing to marry Olivia and help raise the *boppli*."

The bishop and his wife both wore identical stunned expressions.

"But…but…you two hardly know each other," sputtered the church leader.

"Perhaps, but we can both benefit from such an arrangement." Olivia watched as Andrew took a deep breath and plunged on. "The reason this came up is because I found a farm I desperately want to buy, but I don't have enough money for it. But Olivia has money of her own from selling her family home in Pennsylvania. She saw the farm this afternoon and fell in love with it just as much as I did. If we got married, not only could we both have the farm we love, but we could raise Helen in an intact home."

A silence descended upon the room, punctuated only by the ticking of a clock.

Into the tense quiet, Andrew spoke again. "We both want to invest in the farm. That part is not in question. We can draw up the legal documents necessary to become half owners. At first, I had proposed a simple business partnership instead of a marriage. We could both reside on the property, perhaps in separate buildings or another arrangement that would fit propriety. However, we suspected you wouldn't approve, and neither of us wants to do anything that will jeopardize our standing in the church. For that reason, we're willing to make it a marriage of convenience. Either way, I'm ready to help raise the *boppli* and ease Olivia's burden."

Bishop Beiler looked grave. "Andrew, Olivia, you both know as well as I do that marriage is a permanent arrangement. How can you risk entering into such a binding contract without true affection for each other?"

"Bishop Beiler." Olivia met the church leader's eyes. "I am not an attractive woman. I've never been courted. I certainly never expected to have children. I have no expectations of any future romantic match. This arrangement with Andrew suits me just fine."

A pained look crossed the bishop's face, as if he wanted to argue her point but then decided against it.

Fortunately, Andrew chimed in. "And you know my romantic history. I've been avoiding women since Sarah dumped me. Long ago, I decided to focus my efforts on developing a farm. Now it's within my grasp. Olivia is willing to develop it with me, and we each bring our own set of special skills and talents to the table. Together we can make it even more productive than it is now. I also never thought I'd have children of my own, so I'm pleased to help raise Helen. Is that such a bad arrangement?"

"The thing is," added Olivia, "we both have almost identical goals, and the financial means to pull this off. It would also benefit Helen." She tightened her arms around the sleeping baby. "What we lack is your blessing on the arrangement. Neither of us is willing to do anything that would violate our baptismal vows. That's why we wanted to talk to you ahead of purchasing the farm."

To Olivia's surprise, Lois spoke up. "I have no objection," she said. Her voice was quiet and firm. "And you have my blessing to continue."

The bishop's head snapped around to stare at his wife, and Olivia almost laughed at his shocked expression. Evidently, Lois Beiler was not in the habit of making church decisions independent of her husband.

There was a long moment of silence, and then the bishop issued a martyred sigh. "It seems I am outvoted." He fixed a piercing gaze at Andrew, then Olivia. "You have my permission, though I have my reservations. To stop the gossiping tongues, since I know you'll need to proceed on the purchase as quickly as possible, I recommend separate sleeping quarters on the farm until November's wedding month. It would also allow you to get to know each other to some degree before making vows in church. I will expect," he finished sternly, "no indiscretions ahead of time. This is an extremely unorthodox arrangement, and it goes against my better judgment."

"That suits me fine," replied Andrew. "Olivia doesn't deserve to have her name dragged through the mud by any gossip."

Olivia's heart gave a flop at Andrew's regard for her reputation.

The church leader wiped a hand down his face in a gesture that could be interpreted as either weariness or defeat. "A marriage of convenience. Most unusual," he muttered. "Let me pray on it. I am annoyed with myself that I can't think of any objection offhand. What you are asking is not against the *Ordnung* or biblical teachings. But

I have my reservations. You're virtually strangers to each other."

"What finer way of learning more about each other than to get married, then?" Andrew asked in a cheerful tone. Then he sobered. "We're not making light of this situation, Bishop. We're fully aware marital vows are forever. But we both have strong motivation right now—both in raising Helen and in purchasing this farm. I'm confident we can make it work."

"But—and forgive me for asking you both this, but I must—what if you find someone down the line to whom you're attracted?" The church leader looked grave. "Committing adultery is grounds for shunning, as you well know. I have no desire to shun either of you. A business arrangement that precludes any marital affection may work well in the short term. But are you both eager to continue this situation as you grow older? Ten years, twenty years, thirty years from now—will a loveless marriage be enough?"

"I never thought I'd have a marriage at all," Olivia said softly. "To be honest, Bishop Beiler, Andrew's offer is a dream come true. I'm well aware this marriage could stay platonic. But for my entire life, I've been disregarded because of my appearance. If Andrew is willing to overlook that, who am I to argue?"

"And we don't know what the future may

bring," added Andrew. He quirked an eyebrow. "It may not be loveless forever. We may not feel the love of a husband and wife, but perhaps the love of deep friendship. That can carry us through a lot."

The bishop stared at them for a moment, then heaved a sigh of defeat. "Very well. As I said, let me pray on it. You have some time before the sale of the house can go through anyway. I would take that opportunity to ask each other some hard questions."

"Danke," Olivia said gravely. "We will not do anything that will make you regret this."

"Meanwhile," said Lois in a brisker voice, "I'd very much like to see the *boppli*."

"Ach, of course!" Still feeling awkward when removing the sling, Olivia finally extracted the infant, who looked ready to wail at the interruption of her nap.

But Lois was clearly experienced with babies. She took the child and cradled her in her arms, crooning and smiling. *"Ach*, she's lovely."

"Ja, she looks like she'll take after my sister, who has always been beautiful. I just hope I can raise her not to *act* like my sister," she finished wryly.

"In this, having two parents will help," admitted the bishop. He peered at the infant, smiled and seemed a bit more relaxed with his decision.

"I wonder if your sister would have gone astray had your mother been alive to guide her."

"I don't know. I pray for her redemption, but at this point I'm not sure she'll ever come around."

"*Gott* can work wonders," advised the bishop. "Don't give up on her."

Olivia sighed. "I try not to. I must admit to being quite angry with her at the moment. How could she abandon her own child, especially to a woman who has no experience with children? Had Andrew not shown up on my doorstep exactly when he did, I would have been in a full-blown panic. To be truthful, Bishop Beiler, he's a better parent than I am. By a long shot."

"It will work out." Lois handed the baby back to Olivia. "Mark my words."

Andrew walked out of the Beilers' home in something of a daze. The meeting with the bishop had gone far, far better than he'd anticipated. Everything was falling into place. Everything.

"What's the matter?"

He looked over to see Olivia watching him with mild concern. "Stunned, that's all," he admitted. "It's like *Gott* is opening every door to make the purchase of this farm possible."

"*Ja*, it does seem that way." She shifted the baby in the sling. The infant was awake and starting to get fractious.

"I have a feeling there's an intense conversation taking place between the bishop and his wife right now," he continued. "I get the impression it was the last thing he expected—having Lois champion our unusual course of action. He was all set to turn us down. That's why I see the hand of *Gott* in this. How else can it be explained?"

"One of these days, when I know her better, I'd like to have a private conversation with Lois and ask why she did that," Olivia added. "And to thank her too." She gave Helen a little bounce, but the infant was not inclined to be comforted.

"I think I'd better get you home," he said. "It sounds like Helen needs a diaper change and a feeding."

She did, indeed. No matter how much Olivia comforted or bounced the baby, her whimpers morphed into wails. By the time they were back at her cabin, Olivia looked stressed.

"Want me to take her?" he asked as he climbed out of the buggy.

"*Ja*, just long enough for me to get inside and make a bottle of formula." She handed over the crying baby.

"Shhhh," he cooed ineffectively to the infant. He felt under her clothing. "Yep, you need a diaper change. *Komm*, *liebling*, we'll start with that." Seizing the basket of baby things, he followed Olivia into the cabin.

The room was just as messy as before, but this time the chaos made sense in light of Olivia's career, so he ignored it. The work table was already covered with a towel, so he laid the baby on top and swiftly changed her. Olivia mixed formula and prepared a bottle.

At last she sank into the rocking chair, and he handed her the baby. The moment the tip entered her mouth, Helen's crying ceased, and she drank hungrily.

"I still feel out of my depth," Olivia admitted, leaning her head against the rocker's back.

"I think that's normal." He pulled out a kitchen chair and straddled it. "Meanwhile, we have a lot to do in the next couple of days. Since I have the buggy, why don't we go into town after Helen's done feeding and get baby supplies? I'll pay half," he added with a smile. "She's my kid, too, now."

Olivia chuckled. "I'm not completely broke," she said. "*Ja*, I have the lump sum I tucked aside from the sale of *Daed's* farm to purchase a house for myself. But beyond that, I have a decent savings account for day-to-day expenses. I can afford to buy her the baby things she needs."

"Maybe we should set up a joint fund for her," he said thoughtfully. "We can each contribute to it."

"*Ja, gut* idea. But from what Anna Miller mentioned, we'll have some more expensive up-front costs, such as cloth diapers and a few things like a bouncy seat and a crib, but thereafter expenses should be predictable. Mostly we'll have to pay for formula, since obviously I can't nurse her myself."

She looked down at the baby's face. Watching her, Andrew was struck by the fact that this was his future wife. Unless and until she indicated otherwise, it would be purely a contractual agreement. She was plain, as she well knew, but there was a sweetness in her features as she looked at the infant that boded well for a comfortable and agreeable companion.

Mentally, he compared her to Sarah. Certainly, Sarah's features were far more harmonious, but it occurred to him he never saw a similar level of kindness that Olivia seemed to possess innately. He was beginning to think this marriage of convenience might be the start of something. He hoped so. It was a big step—and a big risk—they were both taking.

And yet, could *Gott* be guiding them wrong? Everything was happening fast, but for the good. Andrew was inclined to go wherever *Gott* led him.

Once she was replete, Andrew took the baby over his shoulder while Olivia got ready to go to town. "Got Anna's list?" he asked, patting Helen's back.

"*Ja*, right here. Bless her for writing everything down."

"Then let's go shopping."

The town of Pierce was small, about 3,500 people, and remote from other towns in Western Montana. For this reason, Andrew had found it was well stocked with almost everything anyone could need without having to travel out of the area. While he had never paid attention to baby supplies before, he wasn't surprised that the stores Anna Miller had recommended had everything on the list.

"For an *Englisch* town, they're doing well to accommodate the Amish population," Olivia remarked at one point as he untied the horse from a hitching post that was clearly a recent addition.

"*Ja*, they've been very welcoming, so I'm told." Andrew climbed into the buggy and clucked to the horse. "Most of us live on the settlement, which is a huge ranch that the church bought. There are no *Englischer* living within its boundaries, though a few live just on the edges. The one thing that struck me about Pierce when I first arrived a few weeks ago is how little sprawl there is. The edge of town is just that." He made a chopping motion. "The edge of town. Look, there's Yoder's Mercantile. That's the place you want to sell your baskets."

Olivia peered at the storefront and nodded.

"I met the Yoders at church last Sunday, and they've already invited me to bring in a selection. Nice folks."

"This whole settlement is full of nice folks," agreed Andrew. "I couldn't be more pleased to be here, especially now that I—that *we*—will have a permanent place to live. That was our last stop. Do you want to talk to Eli Miller tonight about purchasing the farm?"

"*Nein*, I'm too tired." She leaned back against the buggy seat and sighed. "It's been an enormously full day, and I didn't get much sleep last night. But you'll see him when you return his buggy and horse, *ja*? You can let him know what we're going to do and how best to get the paperwork in order."

"I can do that." Andrew found himself fired up to get the ball rolling. "In fact, we might be able to move into the house this week. Would that work?"

"*Ja.*" She smiled at him. "Since the Shrocks aren't living there anymore, we can both start moving our things in."

"And I need to make sure the shed is livable for me." He smiled back. "We're going to have a frantically busy rest of the year! Between taking care of Helen and bringing the livestock back in and just settling into the new place and harvesting the crops the Shrocks planted, we'll have our hands full."

"*Gott ist gut*," she replied simply.

"*Ja*, He is," Andrew replied. He directed the horse out of town toward the settlement. "I don't know how we stumbled into this bizarre situation, Olivia, but I'm thankful we did. I'll do well by you and the baby, I promise."

"You're a *gut* man, Andrew." She gave him a shy smile. "I know it was my savings account that was the foundation for this whole arrangement, but the more I think about it, the more grateful I am. I'll also do well by you and try my best to be a *gut* helpmate."

Andrew was feeling pleased and upbeat as the horse headed out of town. It struck him that this arrangement—traveling in his own buggy, with his own horse, his own wife, his own baby, heading for his own farm with its own livestock—would be the regular thing he did the rest of his life.

It was new and unexpected, but he was pleased.

He didn't realize he was smiling until Olivia said, "Penny for your thoughts?"

So he told her. "I'm still marveling," he concluded. "I hope you don't have any second thoughts, Olivia, because at this stage, I don't. Since we have four months until a November wedding, I hope to spend that time proving to you I'll be a *gut hutband* and a *gut vader*."

She chuckled. "Our thoughts are very similar. I know it's just a marriage of convenience, but especially with this little one—" her arms tightened around Helen, asleep in the sling "—it gives me everything I'd hoped for in life. A baby. A man to help. A farm of my own. Well, *our* own. It's more than I ever anticipated, and I'm grateful for it."

He pulled up to the cabin and gave her a grin. "Then let's get this show on the road. I'll go talk to Eli and see what we need to do to make that farm ours." Impulsively, he kissed her cheek, then climbed down from the buggy and went to the other side to assist her. "I'll be by tomorrow, hopefully with more information on the next step."

He carried all their new purchases into the cabin, wished Olivia good-night and headed out the door. It didn't occur to him until he was almost back at the Millers' that Olivia hadn't said much since he'd dropped her off at her cabin and said goodbye. He wondered why.

Chapter Seven

All that evening, Olivia thought about that careless, thoughtless kiss on the cheek Andrew had given her. Even hours later, it still burned an impression on her skin. During the night, snatching some sleep between attending to Helen's needs, she thought about it.

What was she getting herself into? It wasn't that she had any doubts about using her nest egg to help purchase the farm. But would she regret the loveless marriage she had agreed to solely to obtain the farm and provide a helpmate to raise Helen?

That Andrew would be a good father to Helen, she had no doubt. But someday Helen would grow up and leave the nest, and then what? Would she, Olivia, grow to dislike her *hutband*?

During those dark, sleepless hours, when her spirits were at their lowest, she prayed she wasn't making a mistake. And she prayed she would not fall in love with Andrew, who—his romantic history notwithstanding—could easily court a prettier woman and enter into a regular marriage, not a marriage of convenience.

Not for the first time, Olivia wondered why *Gott* had seen to make her so plain. While she didn't especially long for her sister's extravagant beauty, surely He could have spread things out a bit more evenly in the looks department?

But He hadn't, and Olivia had long ago accepted that fact. Or so she thought.

But now... She turned restlessly in bed and pushed her pillow into a more comfortable shape... Now she wondered if or when someone like Andrew could ever see past her face to the lonely heart underneath.

It was an unanswerable question, and by the time Olivia dragged herself out of bed the next morning—with Helen asleep at last—she splashed water on her face and promised herself not to overreact whenever Andrew did anything remotely affectionate.

She made herself breakfast and then sat down to do some weaving before Olivia woke up. Concentrating on her technique, she felt the mildest irritation when she heard a knock on the door, breaking her focus. The irritation turned into anticipation when she realized it could only be Andrew.

But it wasn't. It was a pretty Amish woman about her age, who smiled at her. "Olivia?"

"Ja?" She looked vaguely familiar, and Olivia knew she must have met her in passing at the one church service she had attended so far.

"I'm Eva Hostetler. My *mamm*, Anna Miller, said you could use a little help with a new *boppli*."

Olivia's face lit up. *"Ja!* I'm so sorry I didn't recognize you at first, but..."

"But you've been up all night, right?"

"Right. Please, *komm* in and forgive the mess. Helen is asleep at the moment, and I was trying to get some work done. Would you like some tea?"

"Ja, please." Eva stepped inside, and Olivia saw her eyes dart around the chaos of raw basketry materials.

"I'm a basket-maker," Olivia explained with some embarrassment, compelled to clarify why the room was in such disorder. "Since this cabin is so small, I don't have anywhere to spread out my supplies or do my work. But it looks like that's about to change."

"You *made* this?" Eva touched the unfinished project Olivia had been creating on the kitchen table.

"Well, I'm *making* it." Olivia filled the kettle with water and set it to heat. "Obviously, it's not finished yet."

"Unbelievable." The other woman looked around the room with more attention, taking in the various components. "So you use all this to make baskets." She chuckled. "You should make baskets to hold your various basket-making supplies."

Olivia was stunned. In all the years of perfecting her craft, she had always used the bins her father had made for her. Now that she was here in Montana, it was easier to just pile her raw supplies on the floor or haphazardly on shelves. She had only herself to please, so it didn't matter.

But soon she would be living with someone else. It behooved her to keep her work supplies orderly, even though she would have her own studio. "Can you believe that never occurred to me?" she said in some wonder. "*Danke!* I'm going to do that."

Eva chuckled and seated herself at the table. "So, tell me about the *boppli*. *Mamm* said your sister literally abandoned her own child on your doorstep?"

Olivia brought over the tea things to the table and sat down. She told Eva about the dramatic moment she found her niece. "There are so many coincidences," she concluded, sipping her beverage. "The fact that she was born on the day my *daed* passed away. The fact that she's named after my mother. The fact that she's the grandchild my father never lived to see. There's no question I'll raise her, but since I have no younger siblings, it's been a steep learning curve. Your *mamm*," she added with a smile, "was enormously helpful when I plied her with questions."

"You couldn't have gone to a better person," replied Eva. "When my own *kinner* started coming, she was my rock."

"How many do you have?" inquired Olivia.

"Five." A moment of sorrow dimmed the other woman's eyes. "I lost a few on the way, so each one is precious. *Gott ist gut*."

"*Ja...*" Olivia cocked her head toward the sounds coming from the bedroom. "Sounds like you'll have a chance to meet the *boppli*. Excuse me."

She fetched the baby from her makeshift basket-cradle and brought her out to the living room. "I have new cloth diapers and diaper wraps," she remarked to Eva. "Can you help me figure out how best to use them?"

"*Ja*, of course." For the next few minutes, Olivia got a lesson in cloth diapers as Eva showed her how to fold them and use the diaper wraps, and how to store the soiled diapers until washing. "I'll hold her while you prepare a bottle," Eva concluded.

"*Danke*." Olivia made up a batch of formula while noticing Eva's expert mothering as she calmed the impatient baby. "I hope I'll become as comfortable as you are someday."

"Oh, you will." Without missing a beat, Eva took the prepared bottle and slipped it into the baby's mouth. "By the time you have a *boppli* of your own, this will be second nature to you."

"Ahh..." Olivia paused for a moment. So far no one except the bishop and his wife knew of her and Andrew's upcoming plans. But instinct told her Eva was someone she could trust and confide in, someone who wouldn't gossip or spread salacious rumors. "I don't know if I'll ever have a *boppli* of my own. But let me tell you what's going on..."

For the next half hour, as Eva's eyes widened, Olivia poured out the events of the last few days.

"I've seen the Shrocks' farm," admitted Eva at the end of the recital. "It's stunning. I can understand why you agreed to something like this to buy it. But, Olivia...marriage? A loveless marriage that is little more than a business contract? Are you sure?"

Olivia hesitated. "Maybe *resigned* is a better word," she said. She gestured vaguely toward her face. "I mean, look at me. I've never been courted. I have no idea what it's like to fall in love with a man, much less have a man fall in love with me. What hope do I have of ever getting married except by this oddball method? If Andrew is willing to enter into this contract, then I'm willing too. In fact, I stand to gain a great deal by it, not least of which is providing a father for Helen."

Eva looked down at the drowsy baby. "I suppose I can see that," she admitted. "It's just that…well, my Daniel and I have been so happy, and I want to see others just as happy."

"It depends on what you mean by 'happy,'" replied Olivia. "But I'm grateful. Very grateful. In fact, I marvel at *Gott's* goodness in leading me down this path. And I'll be half owner of the most beautiful farm this side of the Rockies to boot! That's a kind of happiness in my book."

"If you say so." Eva still looked troubled. "But I pray that will be enough."

Olivia warmed to the kind-hearted woman. She could use a friend, and she suspected she had found such a gift in Eva.

"When we're settled in our new place, I'll have you over for tea," Olivia promised. "And then you can see if *Gott* hasn't provided for me despite not giving me a pretty face."

Eva's expression cleared, and she chuckled. "I think you're a lot prettier than you're giving yourself credit for," she said. "And just between you and me, I wouldn't be surprised if Andrew thinks so too."

Thinking about that careless peck on the cheek yesterday evening, Olivia found herself hoping Eva was right. She willed herself not to blush just thinking about it. "Well, I'll leave that up to *Gott*," she replied. "He's done remarkable things so far."

"*Ja*, it sounds like He has." Eva slipped the bottle tip out of the drowsy baby's mouth, snatched up a towel and placed the baby over her shoulder to burp her. "Well, Daniel and I would be happy to help you move when the time comes."

"*Danke*." Olivia looked around at the chaos in the room and mentally planned the size and shape of the baskets she would make to hold her raw materials. "I think I'll put aside some of my consigned orders and start working on storage baskets to make things easier to move. *Gott* willing, I'll need them very soon."

"I'd love to watch you work sometime. I've never seen baskets being made before, though of course I've bought many over the years."

"I've made baskets since I was a child. I have a number of standing wholesale orders, and Mabel Yoder invited me to bring some into their store to sell." She shrugged. "I needed a way to make a living on my own, and making baskets is how I do it. See how *gut Gott* is? He gave me the skills to support myself even without a *hutband*."

"And now you're getting a *hutband* as well." Eva gave her a warm smile. "And who knows what might happen after that?"

* * *

Andrew had a wildly busy day. Spurred on by the financial agreement between him and Olivia, he used Eli's borrowed rig and went into town to begin the necessary paperwork at the title company to purchase the property.

"The purchase should be straightforward," he told the representative. "Cash on the barrelhead, eager seller, no liens, no complications."

"And an eager buyer, it seems," the representative—an older woman—remarked with a smile.

"Ja." He smiled back. "This farm is everything my…my fiancée and I ever wanted." He nearly stumbled over the word. Olivia was, technically, his fiancée…but it sounded strange. "We're both contributing to the price of the property. The sellers had to sell out and go back east for a family emergency. Since they're Amish, it might take longer to communicate with them, but we can put down the money immediately."

"I've worked with a number of Amish families in the last few years, since you've started moving into the area," the woman said. "We're starting to become familiar with the differences involved. Now, because the seller is so far away, there will be some delays, but otherwise I don't anticipate any problems." She hesitated. "How shall I reach you and your fiancée when it's time to sign the paperwork?"

"We can drop in and check," suggested Andrew. "Also, you can leave word with the people who run Yoder's Mercantile, and they can pass it on to me."

"That will be fine." The woman adjusted her reading glasses. "I'll get the ball rolling and let you know when I'll need your signatures."

Andrew turned the borrowed rig back toward the settlement three miles out of town.

He couldn't help but grin. Long ago he had heard an *Englisch* saying: the best revenge is success. With the purchase of this farm, he had "revenged" himself on Sarah and her desertion. He had succeeded in buying a place far prettier than anything he could have afforded back east—and Sarah had missed out on this opportunity when she dumped him.

His thoughts weren't charitable, he knew, but he had spent the last couple of years wrestling bitterness out of his soul. This purchase expunged the rest of his ill feelings.

And he owed it all to Olivia. Thinking about the tall, plain-looking woman who was now his partner—and soon to be his wife—his grin widened. She couldn't hold a candle to Sarah in the looks department, but Olivia far outmatched his former betrothed in kindness and generosity.

He vowed again to himself to be a good father

to Helen and a good husband to Olivia. He owed everything to her. Had she not had the financial means to purchase the farm with him, there was no way he could ever have bought it by himself. He recalled the moment she had virtually yanked him into the house to help with the baby. What a start to their relationship.

He thought about the layout of the farm and wondered how best to handle living arrangements. He was happy to remodel one of the outside sheds into living quarters for himself, since he suspected it would make Olivia comfortable. But what would happen after November, when they were properly married? Doubtless, he would have his own bedroom, since Olivia had expressed no interest in a true marriage.

He was okay with the idea of this being a marriage of convenience rather than a marriage of love. Sarah had burned him badly. This way he was getting a built-in family solely on his terms.

Besides, despite—or because of—Olivia's nature, he suspected she would make a loyal and enthusiastic business partner. And in the long term, was that really such a bad thing?

Hoping Eli Miller wouldn't mind the continued borrowing of the horse and buggy, he bypassed the Millers' farm and continued deeper into the Amish settlement until he came to the Shrocks' place. He turned up the tunneled driveway and marveled again at the sheer beauty of the property when it came into view.

To his surprise, someone was there ahead of him. He recognized the figure of Ephraim King, a respected older farmer known for his immaculate dairy cows. Ephraim was watering the garden as Andrew drove up.

"*Guten tag*, Ephraim," he called. "So you're the one who's been maintaining the property after the Shrocks left?"

"*Ja.*" The older man stopped pumping the hand pump that was attached to the drip-irrigation system to the garden. He pulled out a handkerchief and mopped his face, then eyed Andrew. "What are you doing here?"

Andrew grinned. "You're looking at the new owner of the farm." He climbed down from the buggy.

"*Ach, gut!*" Ephraim looked delighted. "I'm so happy for you, young man. This is a beautiful piece of property."

"*Ja*, I agree." Andrew tied the horse to the hitching post. "We're still doing the paperwork and everything, but I can start taking over the day-to-day chores."

"'We'?" Ephraim cocked his head at Andrew. "But I thought…"

"Olivia Bontrager and I are buying the place together," Andrew explained. Now that he had the bishop's blessing, he didn't see a problem in letting the gossip start. "We'll be getting married in November. In the meantime, I'll be residing in that little outbuilding over there." He pointed.

Ephraim's eyebrows shot up into his hairline, but he said nothing besides a neutral "I see."

Andrew had been so buoyed by the anticipation of owning the farm that he hadn't given much thought to how other church members might respond to the living arrangements. Well, he could blame the bishop—or at least, Lois Beiler—for the unusual situation. A year from now, he told himself, everyone will have forgotten that he and Olivia had started out their married life in such a bizarre manner.

"First comes love, then comes marriage, then comes a baby in a baby carriage," went the *Englisch* rhyme. Whereas he and Olivia were doing it backward: first came a baby, then marriage. Would love follow? He didn't know and, at this point, didn't care.

Ephraim, meanwhile, was walking toward the chicken coop. "I'll show you what I've been doing," he explained, "and then let you take over the chores."

After a brief tour of the coop and the garden, Andrew asked, "What about the livestock, the cows and horses? Are you caring for them?"

"*Ja*. Are you taking them?"

"Absolutely. Let me spend the afternoon getting some things ready, and I'll pick them up tomorrow. Would that work?"

"Ja." Ephraim smiled, and Andrew hoped the older man wasn't holding judgment over him. "It will be nice not to have the extra animals to care for."

"And it will be nice to have my own transportation, since the Shrocks left behind both a buggy and a wagon."

"Well, young man, it sounds like you'll be off to a *gut* start on this property. I'll be off, then."

"Are you walking? I can drive you home," offered Andrew.

"Nein," don't bother. It's not far. I'll just be glad not to have to come twice a day to check on everything."

"Vielen dank" for keeping an eye on the place," said Andrew sincerely.

Ephraim touched the brim of his hat and started down the driveway.

Left alone, Andrew embarked on a leisurely and attentive tour of the property. He started with the shed he intended to outfit for his living quarters. Evidently, it had been used as a guesthouse before, for it was already outfitted with a tiny woodstove and two windows. The walls were insulated. Perfect. He could fit a bed and his personal effects into this space without much trouble and prepare coffee or even cook a meal on the small flat surface of the stove...though he assumed he and Olivia would share meals in the main house most of the time.

He investigated the house next. He unlocked the door and stood in the living room, imagining it furnished with a combination of his and Olivia's possessions alongside what furniture the Shrocks had left behind. He liked what he saw.

With an eye toward bringing the livestock back in the next day, he toured the barn facilities and made sure everything was ready, fences were tight and gates were closed. It was easy to mentally populate the barn, corral and pastures with the three horses and two cow-calf pairs Ephraim had been boarding. He grinned to himself. By this time tomorrow night, the farm would be back up and running.

He wondered how soon Olivia would want to move in. The only thing his vision lacked was a woman to alleviate his bachelor state, and she fit that bill admirably. And a baby as well! Little Helen was darling, and he found himself looking forward to helping care for her.

He decided to swing by Olivia's cabin on the way back to his bunkhouse and ask if she wanted to start moving her things in tomorrow, as soon as he could move the livestock and start using the Shrocks' horse and wagon.

He lingered on the porch for a few last moments, drinking in the sheer beauty of the place. "You're mine, all mine," he whispered, and thanked *Gott* for the woman who had permitted him to acquire what would, he hoped, be the ultimate substitute for Sarah's betrayal.

Chapter Eight

The next few days moved very fast for Olivia. Andrew was fired up with enthusiasm to take possession of the farm as quickly as possible, and she was dragged along in his wake.

"I'm going to start by bringing in the livestock, the horses and cows," he told her the morning after Eva's visit. "That way I can use the Shrocks'—or rather, our—buggy and wagon rather than having to keep borrowing Eli's rig. If you can have your things packed, I can start moving you into the house today, and it means you can stay there with Helen and unpack at your leisure rather than having to keep running back and forth with the baby."

"You're in a hurry," observed Olivia, stuffing willow branches into a hastily made basket to contain them.

"*Ja*, I am. I can't wait to settle in. Don't you feel the same way?"

"I do, *ja*, though having to care for Helen slows me down a bit." She gently chucked the baby under the chin as the infant observed them from her bouncer seat on the kitchen table. "But I will say, it will be nice to have a dedicated spot for my basketry supplies separate and away from where I'm caring for the baby."

The rest of her basketry items didn't have dedicated containers for storage—she hadn't had the time to weave anything else—so she compromised by tying things in bundles and hoping for the best. She spent the rest of the day alternating between taking care of Helen and packing the items she'd need to move to the farm—her bedding, kitchen items, lamps, Helen's cradle basket and other personal effects.

By the time Andrew showed up, driving a beautiful black horse and a wagon, she was ready.

"I don't know her name," he said about the horse as he climbed down from the wagon and stroked the animal's nose. "What do you say to calling her Maggie?"

"Why Maggie?"

"It was the horse I had back in Ohio."

"That's fine with me. Hello, Maggie." Olivia patted the animal on the neck.

"What's the biggest item you have to move?" he asked, heading into the cabin.

"Collectively, all my basket-making supplies, but those can come last since I doubt I'll have a chance to do any work for the next few days." She pointed to the collections of boxes, baskets, cartons and suitcases.

"Will the baby be safe in that bouncer seat while we move things to the wagon?"

Olivia looked at Helen. The infant's eyes were half-closed. "I think she'll be asleep in a few minutes anyway." She grinned at him. "Now's our chance."

Between them, it took half an hour to transfer Olivia's possessions to the wagon. When it was packed to capacity, Olivia lifted the sleeping infant and tucked her in the sling snuggled close to her body while Andrew carried the bouncer seat to the wagon.

The drive to the farm was full of expectation. "Have you moved into the little guesthouse already?" she asked.

"*Nein*, but I'll make do this evening. I'll move the rest of my things tomorrow." He pumped a fist in the air. "Our own farm, Olivia! *Gott ist gut!*"

She chuckled at his enthusiasm. "You really did have it in your mind that a farm would replace a family, didn't you?"

"Completely. And now I have a family, too, of sorts. I can't tell you how happy it all makes me."

What an interesting man Andrew was. He must have been badly hurt by his betrothed's desertion. Yet he was willing to have a marriage of convenience with almost a perfect stranger and become father to a baby he hadn't known for more than a short time.

"It will take us a few days to establish a routine," she said thoughtfully, gazing at the longer shadows as the sun inched down in the west. "Mealtimes, work times, farm chores—that kind of thing."

"I expect I'll be taking care of most of the outdoor stuff," he said, "though I'm not locked into that idea. I want to make sure you have no regrets about this arrangement, so if there's something you absolutely hate doing, let me know and I'll take it over."

"You forget, I pretty much ran *Daed's* farm single-handedly after he lost his strength. I'm *gut* at milking cows and hitching up horses and even plowing."

"And I'm fairly handy in the kitchen and the garden," he countered. "The only thing I never learned how to do was can food."

"I'm a *gut* canner, so I can handle preserving the harvest."

He turned Maggie down the driveway under the tunnel of trees, where her hooves were muffled by pine needles. When he emerged into the evening sunshine again, she drew in her breath. "It's so beautiful."

He pulled the horse to a stop, and they spent a moment in silence gazing at their new home. "*Gott* bless the Shrocks," he murmured. "It must have been painful to give this up."

"*Ja.*" She pointed. "Look, some deer. What a perfect beginning for our stay."

After a few moments, Andrew clucked to the horse and pulled the wagon around as close to the house as he could.

Helen was inclined to fuss, so Olivia kept her in the sling and moved the lighter-weight items while Andrew took care of heavier things. By the time the wagon was unloaded, the log cabin's living room was in chaos.

"It has so much more room!" she exclaimed when Andrew apologized for the confusion. Helen started fussing in earnest. "But I'm going to have to diaper and feed her before doing much else."

"Let me bring in the rocking chair." Andrew manhandled the furniture through the door and set it down on the floor while Olivia rummaged for formula and diapers. "I'll change her while you make up the bottle."

"*Danke.*" She busied herself in the unfamiliar kitchen, mentally arranging it to suit her tastes and needs.

When the baby was dry, Olivia sank down into the rocking chair, took the infant in her arms and began feeding her. Glancing up, she caught an enigmatic expression in Andrew's eyes—a mixture of longing and pleasure at the sight of the baby. Olivia's heart swelled. It seemed he was truly interested in accepting Helen as his own, not just a burden to bear for the broader sake of obtaining a farm.

"Well…" He stepped back. "I'm going to stable the horse for the night and see what last-minute chores need doing."

He disappeared out the front door. Olivia heard him cluck to the horse, and the wagon rolled out of the yard.

She was left alone in the house. The sun had nearly set, and she would need to set up the lamps to provide light as the evenings got much darker. But Helen didn't seem inclined to hurry her meal, so Olivia told herself to be patient. She was eager to explore the house and start organizing things, but it would have to wait until tomorrow.

It was almost fully dark by the time the baby finished her meal, and Andrew came clattering up the porch stairs. "Olivia? Why are you sitting in the dark?"

"Because Helen was feeding this entire time." She tossed a towel over her shoulder and placed the baby in position to burp. "The lamps are in that box there, along with some matches. Why don't you light them?"

Andrew rummaged in the box, and in a few minutes the room was cozily lit with three oil lamps.

"I feel like we should be doing something to celebrate our first night in our home," he remarked with a smile.

"You know, I could tuck Helen into the sling, and we could sit out on the porch," suggested Olivia. "I have a feeling that's going to become a favorite location for both of us after a long day's work."

"Ja, gut." Andrew took one of the lamps and preceded Olivia outside. He placed the lamp on the porch railing while Olivia tucked the baby against her chest in the sling. She was learning that Helen responded well to such a position. The infant seemed to like the feeling of movement as well as Olivia's voice and heartbeat.

"This is nice," she said with a sigh, sinking into a rocker. It squeaked slightly as she set it in motion. "Is this something you can see yourself doing for the next few years?"

"Oddly, yes." Andrew positioned the other rocker in cozy proximity. "I never thought I'd have this privilege—to sit on a porch on my own farm with my future wife and even my own baby."

"Andrew…" Olivia stopped and bit her lip, then plunged forward. "I know this is purely a business arrangement. Will that bother you as time goes on?"

He glanced at her, his eyes unfathomable in the darkness of the late evening. "I don't know," he replied. "For the moment I'm content to let things progress as they may. Will it bother you?"

"Nein," she replied firmly. She patted the baby's back, secure in the sling. "I'm so much richer than I was just a few days ago, even though my bank account is poorer. Or will be, as soon as we pay for the property. Like you, for the moment I'm content to let things progress as they may. *Gott ist gut.*"

It was such a small thing, really...sitting on these porch rockers, watching the twilight on their very own farm. Once, long ago, he had thought to do that with Sarah, experience the quiet contentment that comes at the end of the workday.

Well, Sarah had dumped him... But now he had Olivia. And Helen.

Andrew wasn't sure he liked Olivia's resolution to keep things unchanged between them. The notion startled him, and he took a few moments to explore why. Could it be he was developing...well, affection for Olivia? Affection above and beyond that of a business partner?

He glanced at her through the deepening

gloom. She was certainly nowhere near as pretty as Sarah had been, but she had some things Sarah had lacked. Calmness. Peacefulness. A sense of contentment. Except for that first frantic meeting where she had yanked him into the cabin to help with Helen, he had hardly seen her ruffled beyond the ordinary new-mother frazzles.

Thinking about that first meeting, he suddenly chuckled out loud.

She glanced at him. "What's so funny?"

"Oh, I was just thinking I've never seen you ruffled except for when Helen was dropped on your doorstep and you didn't know what to do, so you almost yanked me inside by my suspender straps."

She laughed quietly, a pleasant sound in the darkness. "I won't say I'm above getting ruffled by caring for a *boppli*. Most mothers, whether by birth or adoption, spend months mentally preparing for the arrival of a child. I had about three seconds."

"That's why I'm impressed. I mean, look at you—you've had Helen for only a few days, and you seem to be adapting so well."

She was silent a moment, then confessed something that took him entirely by surprise: doubts. "I worry, though. Helen, as dear as she is, is so tiny. She certainly won't remember her mother, much less have the opportunity to look to her as an example of behavior. Yet was some part of my sister's personality inheritable? Will Helen someday rebel and leave the faith as my sister did?"

"Nature versus nurture, you mean."

"*Ja*, I guess."

"Is she really that bad, your sister?"

"*Ja. Und nein.* I mean, she's in her early thirties and still can't seem to settle down and grow up. What did her note say? She discovered she wasn't cut out for motherhood and was heading to Europe with her new man." He saw her arms tighten around the baby. "I don't want Helen to be that way."

"You might want to keep that note," he commented.

"The one my sister left with the baby?" she returned, startled. "Why?"

"Because the day may come when she tries to reclaim Helen. That note is proof that the child was abandoned."

"I can't imagine she'll be interested in taking her back." Olivia sighed. "While a huge part of me is furious at what she did—how could she abandon her own flesh and blood?—a little tiny part of me admires the fact that she traveled all the way out here to a remote corner of Montana with the sole and exclusive purpose of dropping her off on my particular doorstep. To me, that means she wasn't entirely heartless in her decision. She knew I'd take the *boppli*. A little part of me admires that."

"I wonder if she'll ever straighten out," Andrew mused.

"I know the bishop suggested I keep praying for her redemption, but frankly, after knowing her for thirty years, I've about given up hope. Oddly enough, I blame her beauty to some extent. She knows she only has to bat her eyes, and men come running. But beauty fades. What will happen when she's fifty? Sixty?"

"Does she have any skills or talents or training?" he asked.

"Some. She learned all the usual things Amish girls learn—cooking and sewing and quilting and such—but beyond that, I don't know. She likes to embroider, and was always *gut* at baking. She briefly had a baking business when she was a youngie until she got bored of it. She's gotten by on a series of jobs, but mostly what she seems to do is glom onto some man and stay with him until one or the other gets tired of the arrangement. Usually, she'd slink home during the interim, weep about her hard lot in life, get bored and then go away again. Rinse and repeat." She paused. "You can understand why it broke my poor *daed's* heart. He went to his grave wondering where he'd gone wrong with her. When I think about that, it makes me even angrier with my sister."

Andrew hadn't meant to open such a painful can of worms for Olivia. As devastating as Sarah's desertion was, it had been mostly his own ego that was hurt. "If your sister *did* decide to reclaim Helen, would you let her?"

"Nein." Her answer was firm and immediate. "Her lifestyle is not the lifestyle for a *boppli*, much less an older child. Helen is now mine. Ours," she added with a smile.

"Ja. And if it comes down to that, I can't imagine a judge would disagree. But just in case, hang on to that note."

"I will."

The call of a great-horned owl echoed across the darkened pastures. "Good thing the chickens are buttoned up for the night," he remarked.

"Ja. Oh, Andrew, it's so *gut* to be back on a farm." In the gloom, he could see the look of delight on her face as she listened to the owl. "When I sold *Daed's* place and moved out here, I had it in my head to settle for a little house on maybe half an acre—just enough room for chickens and a garden. I never thought I'd have a full farm again. I understand why so many people are interested in leaving crowded states behind and migrating here."

"Eli Miller said someone else had been looking at this property too." He gave a wry chuckle. "I hope they won't be too disappointed not to get it."

"How could they not be?"

"*Ja*, true." He changed the subject. "Tomorrow I'm going to keep moving all our household goods in, including all your basketry supplies. I'll take Helen for however long it takes you to set up your studio workshop. After that, we can set up whatever work times you need. The whole advantage of giving Helen two parents is to make sure we each have a chance to get our work done."

He saw the gleam of her teeth in the darkness as she smiled at him. "You're a *gut* man, Andrew."

"*Nein*, I'm not any more *gut* or bad than anyone else. But I always keep my promises, and one of those promises is giving you the chance to get your work done."

"One of the things we'll have to do is decide what things we want to sell to make this farm productive—garden produce or cheese or eggs or dairy products or wheat or whatever. Since we've paid cash for the property, our living expenses should be quite low."

"Maybe we should both talk to the Yoders in town and see what they'd like us to supply. Most of the Amish goods now flow through their store. Besides, didn't Mabel Yoder tell you she wants to see a sampling of your baskets?"

"*Ja.*"

"Then maybe early next week, we can go talk to them. That will give us a few days to settle in here and get an idea of what this place is capable of producing, and what changes we might want to make for next year."

"Such as blueberry bushes. I'd like to plant forty or fifty of them."

"And strawberries," he added. "I suspect fresh strawberries are always in demand in the Yoders' store…"

"And spaghetti squash. I'll bet it will grow well out here."

"And pumpkins. Those are always popular."

With a whimper, Helen began stirring. "I suspect she's getting hungry," remarked Olivia.

"And it's getting late." He rose from his chair. "I can change her if you want to get a bottle ready."

They returned indoors, where Olivia busied herself with mixing a bottle of formula and Andrew changed the baby. "I'm getting better at this," he remarked as he lifted the infant up and snuggled her on his shoulder.

"You were always better at it than I was. Here, I'll take her." Bottle in hand, Olivia sank into the rocking chair. Andrew leaned down to put the infant into her arms. Once the baby was feeding, she looked up at him, her eyes dark in the lamplight. "I've got her for the night. You might want to get some sleep, since I imagine you're wiped out from today's activities."

"*Ja*, I am. *Gude nacht*, Olivia."

"*Gude nacht.*"

Andrew let himself out the back door of the log house and crossed the yard to the ten-by-twelve-foot shed that was his new home away from home until he and Olivia were married. He hastily made up the single bed with clean sheets, tucked the blankets around the foot, then sat down to remove his shoes and change into pajamas.

He *was* tired. Tired but satisfied. He was in the process of acquiring just about everything he'd aimed for in life, in a relatively short period of time.

One thing was certain: his soon-to-be-wife was an easy woman to talk to. Out there, on that porch, their thoughts had just flowed between them. The easy conversation was something he'd never really had with Sarah, and he appreciated the difference.

Except…what would it be like to share the house with Olivia? And maybe even a bedroom?

Chapter Nine

"I think it should go there," said Andrew. "What do you think?"

Olivia rubbed her chin, considering where the antique oak Hoosier cabinet should go. It was by far the heaviest piece of furniture she owned, but it was a cherished heirloom she had transported all the way from Pennsylvania.

The living room was a mess, all their combined possessions heaped in untidy disorder in the main room of the house. They were trying to make order out of chaos.

"That's fine." She chuckled. "Actually, this is rather fun. Once everything is in its place, what a home this will be!"

She should be tired. Between caring for Helen and trying to arrange her new studio workspace and helping Andrew unload wagonloads of their possessions, it was a lot of stress.

Yet, oddly, she felt energized. Some of that energy, she realized, came from her proximity to Andrew.

The man was a workhorse. Olivia had spent her whole life around hardworking men, but it seemed Andrew was among the hardest working she had ever met. Yet he didn't treat work as anything but a blessing, and his positive attitude was infectious.

"You seem happy," he observed now, as together they shoved the Hoosier cabinet against a blank wall in the kitchen. "Is the baby sleeping better?"

"Actually, *ja*." Olivia smiled at Helen, watching everything from the perspective of her bouncy seat on a table in the middle of the room. "She seems to be settling in. I think she was fractious for the first few days because she was getting used to me—to *us*. But even though things are a little crazy with moving here, she seems calmer somehow. She seems to like watching all the activity."

"And getting your own sleep helps a lot, I would imagine."

"*Ja*," she said in a heartfelt voice. "I'll take that," she added, when Andrew picked up a bundle of cattail leaves.

He handed over the materials. "When I first walked into your rental cabin and saw all this organic material scattered everywhere, it made me wonder what was going on. It's not common for an Amish woman to let her surroundings get messy."

"It was just a matter of lack of space," she assured him. She tossed the bundle of cattail leaves in the direction of her studio. "I'm not a slob, truly I'm not. But oddly enough, it wasn't until a suggestion from Eva Hostetler that I had a head-clunk moment. She suggested I make baskets to hold my basket-making supplies. What a concept, right?"

Andrew laughed. She took a moment to admire the teasing look on his face. "That never occurred to you before?"

"*Nein*. Crazy, right? But in *Daed's* house, I had these...these bins, I guess you could call them—" she gestured a shape with her hands "—in which I kept all the different things I needed. So when I transported all my supplies out here, I just had everything piled willy-nilly around the room since I didn't have anywhere to store anything and it was just a temporary arrangement anyway."

Andrew straightened up. "Do you want me to build you bins in your studio?"

She blinked. It hadn't occurred to her to ask him. "*Ja, bitte!* It doesn't have to be done right away, of course, but that would be extremely helpful."

"Look, your work is just as important as my work. *You* have a job to do, *I* have a job to do. If bins will help you do your job more efficiently, then I'll make you some bins."

In that moment, Olivia realized just what a treasure the man was. If she wasn't careful, she could fall in love with him. But good-looking men like Andrew weren't likely to fall in love with a plain woman like her, so she clamped down hard on any such thoughts. *"Danke."* She smiled at him.

Ever efficient, Andrew moved toward the studio. "Let's go take a look at the space. You can give me an idea of what you need."

"Let me grab Helen." Olivia tossed a dish towel over her shoulder, released the straps on the bouncy seat and lifted the baby up. Then she followed Andrew into the studio, stepping over the bundle of cattail leaves she had just tossed.

The room was a lean-to addition to the house with a doorway off the main room. It had clearly been added after the main building was constructed. With windows at either end, the room was about ten feet wide and twenty feet long.

"I was thinking about setting up my worktable there." She pointed to the north window. "Plenty of light, but out of direct sunlight."

"Ja, gut. And I assume your bins would be along this wall?"

"Ja, but keep in mind they don't all have to be the same size. The biggest bins would hold things like willow branches, but I'd also need smaller bins—or maybe boxes—to hold finer

materials such as pine needles. And shelves for the finished baskets before I ship them out."

"What about a shipping station?"

"What do you mean?"

"I mean, when it comes time to pack up your baskets to send them to your wholesalers, would it be convenient to have a specific work spot for that purpose?"

The man was a genius. "I've always just used the kitchen table, but *ja*, that would be wonderful!"

Hands clasped behind his back, Andrew prowled the length and breadth of the room, eyeing the walls. She could almost see the gears turning in his brain.

"Here's what I propose," he said at last. "Let me take measurements of the room. What I'll need you to do is write me a list of everything you'll need a bin, a box or a container for, how many shelves you'll need, what packing supplies you use—that kind of thing. Give me approximate sizes for all the supplies as well. I'll mock it up in a schematic for you to look at, then we can tweak it until you're satisfied."

"I've never had everything in one room before," she admitted, gazing at the empty studio space. "The room I used in *Daed's* house was adequate but certainly didn't have enough space for a shipping area. I stored a lot of materials in a shed, and it meant I always had to dig around to find what I needed."

"Make it your 'dream' studio," he said. "It's worth doing it right the first time."

"*Danke*, Andrew."

They locked eyes for a moment. Olivia was the first to turn away, patting Helen's back as an excuse.

This was, she decided, a good test of marriage. The last couple of days had been a difficult time for Andrew, with multiple trips to assemble their possessions, yet he'd retained his good nature. He was generous too.

And handsome.

"I like doing this kind of stuff," she heard him say with a note of satisfaction in his voice. She turned to see him scanning the wall with an industrial air. "Making the most efficient use of a space and customizing something to a specific purpose."

A tiny part of her recognized that while her feelings for him were changing, evidently his were not. He was just as businesslike as always. *Keep a lid on it, Olivia*, she scolded herself.

"It will feel *gut* to get back to work," she said. "If I can get this little one on a regular sleep pattern, then I can schedule my days better."

"I don't think that's how *bopplin* work," he said with a smile. "I remember my *mamm* having to plan her days around babies, not the other way around. Of course, by that point she could recruit some of us older siblings to help. We'll make it work, Olivia."

"We already have." Composed again, she returned his smile. "Think about it, Andrew. Both of us are benefitting so much from this agreement. Well, all three of us." She dipped her head toward Helen.

"Well, back to it, then." He moved past her into the main room of the house. Olivia followed and tucked Helen back in the bouncy seat.

"Bookcases," he said, pointing to a spot on the wall. "I have a fair number of books. Do you?"

"*Ja*, some. Enough to fill a *gut*-sized bookcase."

"Then I'll wait to build shelves until I know how many we both have. But let's reserve that wall space for bookshelves.

"What about a pantry? I'm kind of surprised this home wasn't built with one."

"*Ja*, me too." Andrew rubbed his chin, considering. Then he pointed. "What if, instead of bookshelves right there, I box in a long, narrow room against that blank wall for a pantry? Then we can put bookshelves against the pantry wall. That way we can kill two birds with one stone."

"I like that!" Immediately, Olivia could see the advantage of his idea. "It would be close to the kitchen too. That would give us a lot of bang for the buck, in terms of efficiency."

"This house is fine for a family, but it's small enough that I doubt it will ever be used for church services," he remarked. "Since it doesn't have a cellar, it means we'll have to make everything as space efficient as possible."

"It will probably take us a year to get everything to the order we want it. But we'll cope in the meantime."

Olivia was aware of something changing between them. Andrew was planning for the future with enthusiasm. There seemed to be a dawning friendship and warmth between them, with gentle teasing and humorous sparring as they decided how to fix up the house.

It boded well for the future.

"I think I'll start on building up your studio first," Andrew remarked. He forked some scrambled eggs into his mouth.

They were sitting at the kitchen table over a late and hastily assembled dinner of eggs and toast. A single oil lamp illuminated the kitchen. Helen, fed and diapered, sat in her bouncy seat like a centerpiece amid the dishes.

"Why?" asked Olivia. She seemed genuinely puzzled. "There are a lot of things to do. I would think my studio would be a lower priority. I can still get work done."

"*Ja*, true, but a project is a project. It's not like we bought a fixer-upper. I don't need to build much by way of infrastructure. But I want to make this place shine. It's my first time being a homeowner."

"Then *ja*, I would be grateful to have a studio in order."

"I can't do anything tomorrow, since it's Sunday. Think of it! We'll be going to church with our own horse and buggy!"

"And raising a few eyebrows." She gently waggled Helen's little foot. "I hope the bishop will make an announcement about how Helen came along, as well as this arrangement he's allowed us to have. Otherwise, we might be ruffling some feathers."

"Nervous?" he asked, even though it hadn't occurred to him before.

"*Ja*, a little. I'm new to this community. So are you. I don't want to give people the wrong impression about me. About us."

"It's the bishop's responsibility to quell any rumors that might spring up," he replied firmly. "That's his job, and he *did* give us permission for this arrangement."

Unexpectedly, she giggled. "I still remember

the look on his face when Lois spoke first. *She's the one who really gave us permission.*"

He chuckled, enjoying the glint of humor in her eyes. "He did look surprised."

"It makes me wonder…" She crunched into a piece of toast. "Why did Lois jump in like that? What did she see that the bishop didn't?"

"What do you mean?"

"I mean…it was like she had some sort of feminine intuition and was able to grasp something, to see something, her husband didn't, at least at first. He was going to flat out refuse us until she jumped in."

"Then it's up to him to defend his actions to the church community and support us." Andrew gulped down some milk and wiped his mouth. "That means quelling any gossip or rumors. Besides, a year from now it will all be water under the bridge. The farm will be ours legally and we'll have been married with a proper church wedding, and life goes on. Neither of us has a bad reputation we need to hide, so it's not like anyone can attack our character. Sometimes *Gott* just throws strange things in our paths, and we have to adapt."

"I hope everyone else in church agrees. It's also the first time I'll have Helen in a church service. What will I do if she starts fussing?"

"You know what I suggest? Sit next to an experienced mother, maybe Anna Miller or Eva Hostetler. Either one can guide you."

"*Gut* idea!" Her face brightened, then sobered. "I hope I'll make a *gut* mother. I never had an example."

He was puzzled. "Maybe not from your own mother, but surely you've watched how women raise children all your life?"

"*Ja*, but it's different when it's your own child. I want to do well by Helen. I don't want to raise her to become like her *own* mother."

"'Forewarned is forearmed,' as they say. We'll both guide her toward a Plain lifestyle."

She sighed. "Andrew, I'm so grateful you're here to help raise her. Growing up without a mother was hard. But in some ways it's harder to grow up without a father."

"We're both being plunged into responsibilities we didn't foresee," he admitted. "Yet *Gott* gives us strength to rise to the occasion. All we have to do is let Him guide us. I don't know how to be a father any more than you know how to be a mother, but I figure that will come as Helen gets older. *No one* enters parenthood for the first time knowing exactly what to do."

She gave a rueful chuckle. "*Ja*, you're right. But most Amish women have grown up around *kinner*, and often have their own mothers or sisters there to guide them."

"There isn't a single woman in church who won't step in to guide you, starting with Anna Miller and Eva Hostetler. Or even Lois."

An awkward noise from Helen, followed by a noisome smell, indicated dinner was over. Andrew chuckled. "I'll take care of her," he offered.

"*Danke*. I'll wash up."

He lit a second oil lamp and moved it into the living room. Even though the house was still in some disorder, Andrew knew exactly where all the diaper supplies were located. Helen had made a mess of her garments, but that didn't faze him. Within ten minutes, he had the baby clean and fresh and attired in a fresh gown. She looked content during this process, and looking at the baby's dark eyes, Andrew knew he was starting to fall for the charms of the infant.

Then her facial expression changed, and he recognized the signs of hunger. "I'm going to feed her," he said. Hitching her over his shoulder, he made a bottle of formula while Olivia washed dishes.

"I still think you're better at this than I am," she said with a smile, glancing at him.

He sat down in the rocking chair, cradled the baby in his arms and put the bottle to her mouth. Immediately, her fussing ceased, and she ate eagerly. "I have some advantages over you in terms of experience," he admitted. "And at least I can feed her, since she's a bottle baby."

"You're going to be a *gut vader*, Andrew." She returned to her washing.

Andrew was warmed by her praise.

He examined Olivia from behind as she was occupied with her task. She was a tall woman, and slim. Her movements as she worked were efficient. She was no-nonsense and forthright, clever and witty, hardworking and affectionate with the baby. Except for her lack of conventional beauty, she was, in every way, an exemplary woman.

What fools were the young men in her old church that they'd never recognized Olivia's assets? Or were they all, as he had been with Sarah, blinded to her qualities by the physical beauty of her prettier sister?

That, of course, had been his own failing, and he'd paid for it. But that was the failing of all young men, he knew. It was instinctive to seek out the pretty, not the plain. But how many men went through and married their own version of Sarah, only to regret it down the road when the face didn't match the heart?

He understood now how he had dodged a bullet with Sarah. The man she had chosen over him was welcome to her. But now, by some strange twist of providence, he found himself with a woman who was Sarah's polar opposite...and more and more, he found himself intrigued by Olivia as more than just a business partner.

She finished stacking the dishes in the drain rack, dampened a dish towel and wiped down the table. With the kitchen in order, she wiped her hands dry, smoothed her apron down and came to join him as he finished feeding the baby.

"She's just as content in your arms as mine," she observed.

"She's just hungry," he countered with a smile.

Their eyes locked for a moment, until she skittered her gaze away. In the lamplit room, he saw her blush.

Blush? Really?

With a small grunt, Helen fell off the bottle. He handed it over to Olivia as he put the baby over his shoulder to burp her. "That should do her through the night," he observed.

"*Ja. Danke*, Andrew. She's sleeping mostly through the night, now, almost like she's getting on a schedule."

"I'm going to get an early start on the chores," he said. "We'll have to leave for church around eight in the morning, since I want to be there to help set up."

"I feel bad I won't be able to contribute much to the meal afterward," said Olivia. "But I'll make it up during the next service. Here, I'll take the baby."

She leaned down and gently lifted the sleepy infant off his shoulder. He caught a whiff of soap and a hint of the rosemary she had added to the scrambled eggs—an attractive combination. He stood up from the rocking chair and subtly watched her as she cradled the infant and crooned to her. Yes, she was a good mother.

"I'll say *gude nacht*, then." He didn't want to leave but knew he must.

"*Gude nacht*, Andrew."

Without any excuse to linger, he let himself out the back door and made his way to the little outbuilding that was his bachelor quarters until the proper wedding in November, as agreed.

Later, he lay in bed, hands stacked beneath his head, and stared at the dark ceiling of the small room. This was just the first of what would be an endless series of domestic evenings—having dinner, sharing chores, making small talk.

Having been a reluctant bachelor for so many years, he found himself cherishing these small moments. He cherished the memories from his own childhood when the evening chores were finished and his parents and siblings were scattered around the room, engaged in reading or puzzles or board games or other occupations. His parents were happy and compatible with each other, and unconsciously he longed for that same level of contentment in his own future.

The bitterness of Sarah's desertion was starting to fade as Olivia took her place. Could it be that *Gott* had provided him with that domestic contentment he wanted after all?

As he drifted off to sleep, a thought crossed his mind. Why had Olivia blushed when she met his eyes?

Chapter Ten

Olivia got up early, leaving Helen asleep in the basket-cradle in her bedroom, to try to cobble together some food for the potluck meal after the church service. Especially because she was so new to the community, it galled her to go empty-handed.

Wondering what to make, she stepped into the garden and saw ripe broccoli heads, and it gave her an idea. Fetching a basket and a knife and taking a quick peek at the baby to make sure she was still asleep, she returned to the garden and cut some broccoli, pulled a red onion and harvested a small cabbage.

By the time Andrew came into the house carrying two buckets of fresh milk, she had pulled together a cold broccoli salad tossed with a few raisins and a dressing. She also whipped up some biscuits and gravy for breakfast.

"What's this?" Andrew inquired, pinching a piece of broccoli and gesturing toward the salad.

"My dish for the potluck. *Danke* for the milk. I'll get it strained."

"And I —" he cocked his head, listening "— will go take care of Helen."

"Ja, gut."

He disappeared into her bedroom. It was a little embarrassing to have him fish the baby out of the basket-cradle in her own private space, but Olivia knew she would have to get used to such casual intimacies.

He reemerged in a few moments with the fractious baby. "Shh, shh, *liebling*," he cooed to her. "*Ja*, you're wet. I'll get you changed, and then a nice bottle…"

Olivia had to blink back sudden tears. So far, Andrew was making out to be a good father.

"I have a feeling Helen is going to be the talk of the town," she remarked as Andrew settled in the rocker to feed the baby. "Most *bopplin* that are born in the church are expected and anticipated. This one? Not so much."

"Maybe not, but I couldn't be more happy to be her *daed*." He looked down at the infant's face as she fed. "When Sarah left me, it's like she stole away any future *kinner* we might have. I went a long time thinking I wouldn't have one of my own. I'm glad to have Helen."

The moisture was back in Olivia's eyes. She turned away to stir the biscuit gravy on the stove.

An hour later, with Helen tucked snug in the sling, she handed up the basket of food to Andrew and climbed into the buggy.

"Driving our own rig. Guiding our own horse," he remarked. "I thought it would be a long time before I had any of these things. *Gott ist gut.*"

"*Ja,*" she agreed, looking around at the sparkling morning. At the moment, it seemed impossible for anything to go wrong.

As they approached the home of the Stoltzfus family, who was hosting the church service, more and more buggies could be seen, as well as families walking. Olivia still didn't know many people—this was only her second church service—and for a moment she felt a bit shy. She noticed a couple of startled glances, though whether it was because she was riding with Andrew or because she had a baby in her arms, she didn't know.

Following other buggies, Andrew guided the horse to where families were discharging, with children climbing down from wagons and women carrying baskets of food along with a few babies. He paused while Olivia disembarked. "I can carry the basket of food as well as the diaper basket after I park and unhitch," he offered. "I can meet you over there." He pointed to a tree.

"*Ja, gut,*" she returned, trying not to feel out

of place among the crowds without the support of his presence.

She went to stand next to the tree. Helen was quiet in the sling, and Olivia watched the ebb and flow as families prepared for the worship service. While there was some quiet talk, the air was subdued. Socializing came after the church service, not before.

"*Guder mariye*, Olivia," said a voice.

Olivia turned and saw Eva Hostetler, who had three little girls with her. "*Guder mariye!*" she exclaimed, delighted to see the other matron.

"Are you sitting with anyone?" Eva asked. "If not, you're welcome to sit with *Mamm* and me."

"*Vielen dank*, I'd like that." She added, "I still feel a little awkward by myself. But I'll need to wait for Andrew since he has the diaper basket."

"How's this little one?" Eva spent a moment cooing over the infant.

"I see you're using the sling," remarked Anna Miller as the older woman walked up.

"*Ja*, and I see why you recommended it," replied Olivia, smiling. "It makes things so much easier."

"Olivia is sitting with us," Eva told her mother.

"That way, if Helen starts fussing, I'll have moral support," joked Olivia.

She saw Andrew heading toward them, two baskets in hand. "Looks like everyone's filing in," he said, referring to people moving to seat themselves in the large barn in which the service was being held.

Olivia received friendly nods from other church-goers, and not a few startled glances at the baby. It was understandable. Two weeks ago she was a spinster. Now she was a mother, and soon to be a wife.

The service proceeded like most church services: hymns, an introductory sermon, prayers, scripture readings, the main sermon given by the bishop, testimonies, closing prayers. Olivia was proud of Helen for sleeping through almost the entire thing. Only once did the baby wake up, and some gentle patting and bobbing managed to lull the infant to sleep again.

However, when the bishop stood up to make announcements, she knew it was time to attend to Helen's needs. She hoped the church leader didn't have much more to say.

"I'd like you to welcome the newest addition to our community," he began, and to Olivia's surprise, he outlined, with remarkable accuracy, the unexpected circumstances of Helen's arrival and why Olivia had chosen to keep her. Heads turned to look, and Olivia smiled self-consciously and gave an exaggerated pat of the sleeping baby in the sling. She knew she would be surrounded by women after the service, all anxious to meet the *boppli* who had been dumped on her doorstep.

But then the bishop continued. "Olivia understands the difficulty of raising a *boppli* on her own, and so she and Andrew Eicher are joining forces to raise the child together," he said. "They've pooled their funds to purchase the Shrocks' farm and are staying in separate quarters on the property until their wedding in November." It might have been Olivia's imagination, but she thought she heard a note of defensiveness in the bishop's tone of voice.

A slew of startled whispers started up among the congregants. For a moment, Olivia thought the hum of voices signaled approval.

And then a thin trickle of horror ran through her. It wasn't *approval*—it was shock and *dis*approval. The smiles that had been turned toward her dropped away.

She met Andrew's eyes across the room. He looked equally concerned. But it was too late; nothing could be changed.

Suddenly, the easy arrangement of rushing into a marriage of convenience—even with the benefits it brought her—seemed a high price to pay. These were now her people. She wanted their good opinion. By focusing only on the advantages of this arrangement—co-ownership of the farm, a valuable helpmate in Andrew and a father figure for Helen—she had disregarded the other, less tangible but just as important detriments.

"Apparently that didn't go over well," Eva whispered next to her.

So she wasn't imagining things if Eva had picked up on the same disapproving mood. *"Ja,"* she murmured back. "I just hope everyone understands the bishop gave us his blessing for this arrangement. We specifically did that because we didn't want to jeopardize our standing in the church."

Anna overheard them. "It'll pass," she advised quietly. "Least said, soonest mended."

The maxim might apply to an embarrassing one-time blunder like tripping over a tree root, but not necessarily to two unmarried—yet baptized—people deliberately flaunting their living arrangements for the next few months until their relationship could be legitimized in the eyes of the church.

She bit her lip as people rose to their feet and began filing out of the barn. Everyone avoided looking at her, except—bless them—Eva and Anna, who stayed firmly next to her in solidarity, including Eva's three daughters. Olivia knew these two women were highly regarded in the community, and she drew strength from their support.

Left almost alone, she rose from the bench, stiff from sitting for so long, and felt Helen's diaper. "I need to change her," she said to Eva. "Where's a good place?"

"There's a spot outside under a tree I often use," Eva suggested. "*Komm*, I'll show you."

Olivia snatched up the diaper basket while Eva, shepherding her daughters ahead of her, led the way out of the barn. "You may go play now, *kinner*," she told them. "*Komm* back to me when it's time to eat." The children scampered off.

Anna and Eva led her to the grassy spot, and Olivia laid a blanket on the ground and quickly changed the child's diaper. She felt like weeping. Suddenly, it seemed her reputation was shredded, all because she and Andrew had made a series of decisions based purely on business advantages.

Anna seemed to pluck her thoughts from the air. "Don't let it worry you, *liebling*," she said. "If you sought the bishop's approval ahead of time, you haven't done anything wrong."

"Then I hope he makes that clear to the rest of the congregation," she replied. With the baby now clean and fresh, she leaned her back against the tree trunk and fished out a premade bottle to feed the infant. "*Vielen dank*, both of you," she said with a tremulous smile. "I'm going to sit here and feed Helen. You go get some lunch."

"*Komm* eat with us when you're finished," said Eva, standing up next to her mother.

"I will, *danke*."

Her new friends departed. Olivia looked after the two women as they walked toward the tables where the lunch food was spread out, and she wondered if they were the only friends she'd ever have here in Montana.

Andrew felt the temperature in the barn drop many degrees after the bishop explained the living arrangements between him and Olivia. The low murmur of men's voices around him sounded shocked, and he was conscious of some inscrutable looks, though most of the other men refused to meet his eyes.

He was dismayed...and annoyed. Really, was it anyone's business how he and Olivia conducted their private life? It wasn't like they were doing anything wrong...

But a moment later, his annoyance faded. As strict as these social norms were, they played a vital part in maintaining the cohesion of the community. And the strength of the church community, he knew, was the lifeblood of his faith. Without it, he could be cast adrift, anchored by his beliefs in *Gott*, but without a moor to keep his boat from bobbing wildly on the waves.

Concerned, he met Olivia's eyes across the

room and realized she felt the change in atmosphere as well. In a somber frame of mind, he rose to his feet and prepared to file out of the barn with the other men.

Outside, he saw Olivia, flanked by Anna Miller and her daughter, Eva Hostetler, moving to a spot under a tree, where she laid the baby on a blanket and changed her diaper.

He lingered alone until the other women left to go eat, then he joined Olivia under the tree, where Helen was hungrily drinking a bottle. "That was awkward," he said in a low voice.

"Ja." She blinked hard, and he realized she was close to tears. "What do we do now?"

"I don't know." Morosely, he looked at the groups of chattering people, many laughing and smiling, children darting around, and realized how much he craved the stability and approval they provided. "I wish I could make everyone understand we did this with the bishop's approval."

"They know. He wouldn't have explained our arrangement, otherwise. The problem is, they still disapprove."

He slumped on the grass next to his future wife and watched as she fed his future child. When did everything get so complicated? Sure, he'd gotten everything he wanted—but at what price?

"I have a feeling," he mused glumly, "that Bishop Beiler is having second thoughts, but having allowed us to do this, he might be... No, he wouldn't do that," he corrected himself. "I was about to say he might be spreading rumors about us, but of course he wouldn't."

"*Nein*, I don't think he has to," replied Olivia. The baby gave a little grunt and fell off the bottle. Olivia put a towel over her shoulder and placed the baby on it, giving her back some pats. "But his tone of voice conveyed a lot of unspoken feelings. Or maybe it was just my imagination."

"*Nein*, it wasn't just your imagination. I thought the same thing." He heaved a sigh. "Shall we go get something to eat?"

"*Ja*." She started to climb to her feet, the baby still over one shoulder, and without thinking, he extended his hand to assist her up.

Their eyes locked as she placed her hand in his. After pulling her to her feet, she was nearly as tall as he was. He stood for a moment, still holding her hand, until she pulled away and dropped her gaze to the ground. He saw her cheeks stain red.

She's blushing again, he thought... And somehow, despite the complications of the last few minutes, that pleased him.

"Anna and Eva invited us to sit with them,"

she said, and her voice sounded controlled. She reached down for the sling and pulled it over her head, adjusting it around Helen's little body until the baby was snug against her chest. "At least we know we won't be among hostile company."

"Well, *hostile* might be too strong a word," he said lightly, starting to walk toward the food tables. "*Disapproving*, perhaps."

"Either way, it's uncomfortable. I'm grateful the Millers and Hostetlers are welcoming."

They filled plates with food and then went to join the others. Anna and Eli Miller sat with Eva, her husband and assorted children.

"Have you met my *hutband*, Daniel?" asked Eva.

"*Ja*, I have. *Gut* to see you again." Andrew shook the man's hand.

"And I'm Olivia Bontrager," added Olivia, shaking his hand. She angled her body a little. "And this is Helen. She's fed and changed, so she's happy now."

"Now, why did you two move to your new place without letting us help out?" Eva gently scolded before biting into a piece of cold fried chicken.

"We just got too busy," Andrew replied after a sip of lemonade. "But we're pretty much settled in now. In *separate quarters*," he emphasized, trying to keep any trace of bitterness out of his voice.

"I figured as much." Daniel calmly bit into a biscuit. "Don't let the gossip bother you."

"But it does," he admitted. "I don't want misconceptions about our situation."

"What's it like?" asked Eva. "The farm, I mean. Is it everything you hoped for?"

"Ja!" Relieved to have the conversation change to his favorite subject, Andrew grinned like a schoolboy. "Very much so. We got the Schrocks' livestock back from Ephraim King, so we have cows, a pair of draft horses and Maggie the buggy horse."

"He's been working nonstop," added Olivia. "In addition to the barn chores, he's going to build me organizational bins and places for all my basket-making supplies."

"The property is beautiful," Andrew continued. "Such a *gut* layout, and an excellent ratio between pasture, hayfields, grain fields and a woodlot. I just couldn't ask for anything more..."

Buoyed with enthusiasm for his new home, Andrew tamped down his pride. *Hochmut*. He didn't want to come across as boastful of *Gott's* blessings.

It wasn't until the end of the potluck, when families were collecting both children and dishes, that Andrew had an idea. It might be a possible solution to the issues he and Olivia faced. He tucked the thought into the back of his mind.

He went to hitch up the horse to the buggy while Olivia collected baskets and dishes, jostling with other men to get the animals to the correct vehicles. When Maggie was properly hitched, he found Olivia and carried the food basket and the diaper basket while she carried Helen tucked in the sling.

It was the same courtesy he had seen countless men perform for their wives countless times during his life, and now it was his turn to do the same with his woman and his baby. Despite the uncomfortable undercurrents of the afternoon, he found he liked this new role.

Once in the buggy, heading down the road toward the farm, he broached the subject that was on his mind. "So. Since it seems apparent that this arrangement isn't meeting the approval of anyone else in the church, I think we're going to have to make a change."

"What kind of change?" She hugged Helen, tucked firmly against her chest.

"I was in such a rush to secure the farm that I didn't really give much thought to the example we might be giving to other youngies who are courting," he explained. "To redeem our reputation, I think I'd better move out until November."

She sucked in her breath and stared ahead at

the road, then nodded slowly. "Or I could. The farm needs you more than it needs me at the moment, and Helen needs me more than she needs you at the moment. If we're going to separate, I'm the more logical person to move out. I can go back to the cabin I was renting."

"This is just so...so *schtupid*," he said in frustration. "We were just developing a *gut* working arrangement. Everything would be easier with two people working toward the same goal. But I suppose that's how coveting works—the item is gained, but at a price. And the price we're facing is either our reputations—and how it might reflect on Helen in the future—or one or the other of us moving off the property until November."

"We haven't paid for the property yet," she reminded him, "though that will change this week, when the cash goes into escrow and we sign the paperwork. But for now, our money is still our own. We could give up the farm and just go back to what we were doing."

He felt a clutch of despair at the thought of losing everything he had so suddenly gained. "Is that what you want to do?" he asked bleakly.

"Nein!" Her answer was immediate. "I suppose I'm just as gripped by the sin of coveting as you are. I don't want to lose that property. There's something about it that just feeds my soul. I could easily stay there the rest of my life."

"*Ja*, me too. Then we've got to figure out a way to satisfy propriety as well as proceed with the purchase." He slumped in the seat of the buggy, reins loosely clasped in his hands, and tried to think.

"There is one more option…"

He almost didn't hear her, the words were so quiet. He glanced over and saw the stain of blush was back in her cheeks. "What's that?"

"What you suggested earlier. We could get married sooner. Right away. This week, even."

Chapter Eleven

Olivia didn't know where she'd found the courage to make such a brazen suggestion, but in her eyes it was the only way she and Andrew could recapture their tattered reputations, as well as allow them to both stay on the farm.

And if there was another reason behind her proposal, she refused to examine it too closely.

She saw Andrew frown. "It's barely August. People would talk if we got married before November."

"People are talking anyway. We're already going in together financially, to the point where we will be linked together for years, if not for life. What difference does it make if we formalize that arrangement in the church sooner rather than later?"

Her heart beat rapidly as she waited for his response. "I suppose we could go talk to the bishop about it," he conceded. "But if he says *nein*, then do you still want to help finance the farm?"

"*Ja.*" She looked up and could see the end of

their driveway ahead. "We've been on it for just a couple days, and already it feels like home. I want this farm every bit as much as you do, Andrew. And it will be a fine place to raise Helen, and…and…" She trailed off and bit her lip.

Andrew glanced at her sharply, but he didn't probe about what she didn't say. And that was a good thing, since she'd almost said, "And any other *kinner* we may have."

Andrew considered a marriage of convenience to be just that: convenient. It was a means to an end, a way to achieve a goal, an opportunity to co-own a magnificent piece of property. It was only she who was assigning a greater meaning to the arrangement, the chance for a true marriage and—possibly—future children of their own.

But he didn't need to know about that. She would keep that secret locked inside herself until the day she died. A loveless marriage to a kind man was better, she thought, than no marriage at all. *Gott* had seen fit to deprive her of beauty, but in His goodness, He had still provided her with a *hutband*. Perhaps love wasn't necessary… at least on Andrew's part.

"Then let us do this. Tomorrow let's go into town. We can stop first at Yoder's Mercantile so you can drop off your basket samples, then go to the title company to deposit the money into the escrow account and sign the paperwork for the farm. On the way home—*after* signing the paperwork, mind you—let's go straight to Bishop Beiler's place and see what he thinks about an earlier wedding. But even if he says *nein*, we'll have already signed the escrow papers, which will commit us to purchasing the farm."

"Ja, gut." She snuggled Helen closer and admitted, "I can't begin to tell you how much this all agrees with me. The farm offers a sense of permanence I never thought I'd have. After *Daed* died, as you know, I planned to buy something small. But I realize now I would have missed the independence a full-scale farm would have offered, a place where we can produce everything from our own cheese to our own firewood."

"Me too," he replied, his hands loose on the reins. "It's what I visualized with Sarah. I had it in my mind that 'the best revenge is success,' though revenge is certainly a concept not encouraged in our church. But a farm is a lonely place for just one person. It's a place where both the work and the pleasure should be shared. I—I'm glad to have you along for the journey, Olivia."

The hitch in his voice surprised her. She knew he was fixated on possessing the farm. But now it sounded like her contribution went further than merely financial. It sounded like he wasn't harboring any doubts about the prospect of marrying her. It was a good sign...even if it meant just a slightly more personal aspect of a business deal than most people ever experienced.

He slowed the horse and directed it through the tunnel of trees toward the house. As always, Olivia felt a tiny frisson of gladness when she saw the dramatic parting of vegetation to where the house sat, tidy and welcoming, on its jeweled lawn of grass.

She glanced upward as Andrew guided Maggie toward the barn. "I do believe it's going to rain," she said in some surprise. She pointed to clouds mushrooming up into the southwestern sky.

"*Ja*, looks like you're right!" He also sounded surprised. "We've been driving away from the clouds, and I didn't notice. I think I'll prepare all the animals to get buttoned up early."

"I'll help." The moment he pulled the horse to a stop, she climbed out, clutching Helen in the sling.

"Are you sure?" he asked doubtfully. "How much can you do while holding a baby?"

"Not as much as you," she retorted with a smile. "But I'm not helpless. Tell you what, I'll take care of the chickens."

"*Ja, gut.*" A gust of wind surprised them, and she recognized the signs of a fast-moving storm cell.

They separated for their various tasks, with

Andrew disappearing into the barn with the horse still hitched to the buggy. Clutching her *kapp* so it wouldn't be yanked off by the wind, Olivia went into the chicken yard, where the birds clucked and ran around as if sensing the change in weather. She made sure their feeder and waterer were full, collected eggs in one of two small baskets she kept in the coop, and made sure the gate was closed behind her. She took a quick tour around the garden, but everything seemed able to withstand wind and rain, so she came back into the house.

However, she remembered the diaper basket and food basket were still in the buggy, so—still holding Helen in the sling—she trotted out to the barn. The wind continued to rise, and the clouds blocked the sun, causing the temperature to drop.

Inside the barn, Andrew was pitching some grass hay into feeders for the horses and cows. "I'm going to leave the barn doors open so the animals can come in as they please," he told her. "But I'll just leave the calves on the cows for the night, which means no milk for us. Is that okay with you?"

"*Ja*, sure." She reached into the buggy to retrieve the baskets. "We have plenty of milk in the icebox, and I had no plans to make cheese anytime soon."

"Then I'll be in in a few minutes."

"Better hurry." She peered out the barn door. "Those clouds are moving in."

She went back to the house and felt the first drop or two of rain. The wind whipped the branches of the oak and maple trees in the yard and rustled the pine and fir trees on the edges of the pasture, but the porch was a safe haven. She stood and watched the show. Helen was awake but quiet. "Quite the storm, eh, *liebling*?" she asked, angling her body so Helen had a clearer view of the tempest. The baby's eyes stayed focused on her, however.

Andrew came dashing out of the barn just as the rain began pelting down. He sprinted across the yard and up the porch steps, laughing as his shirt got wet. "That came on fast!"

"Our first rainstorm in the new house." She stood for a moment, looking out at the rain. "I'm going to put the kettle on for tea before changing and feeding Helen. Then what do you say to sitting here and just watching the weather?" She gestured toward the porch rockers.

"I'll change Helen," he offered. "And I can feed her out here as well as in the house."

She realized Andrew enjoyed the time spent rocking on the porch as much as she did. While she made tea, from the corner of her eye, she watched as he cooed and teased Helen during the diaper change. She put tea things on a tray while he prepped the bottle, and then they went outside, where the wind and rain presented a dramatic tableau from the calm shelter of the sturdy porch.

"From what I gather, storms like this only happen a few times during the summer," Andrew remarked, sinking into a rocking chair. He crossed one foot across the other knee and propped the baby up, then slipped the bottle into the baby's mouth. "We might lose a fir tree or two."

"Then that will become next year's firewood." She poured his tea and put the mug at his elbow on the little table between them, then decided to voice something that was bothering her. "Andrew—even if the bishop agrees to an earlier marriage, will it be enough to thaw the attitude of everyone in church?"

"Will it bother you if it doesn't?"

She was startled at his question. "Well, *ja*. Of course. *Gott* willing, we'll be living here the rest of our lives. We may not be shunned, since we embarked on this project with the bishop's permission, but it was an uncomfortable feeling having everyone be so standoffish."

"Except the Millers and Hostetlers. They were friendly and welcoming as always. And those are some very influential people here on the settlement. Don't worry about it, Olivia. Everyone will come around, especially once we're married."

"I suppose." She gazed out at the drenched lawn. "I don't like being the subject of gossip."

"We've given them nothing to gossip about." He spoke with confidence, but Olivia wasn't so sure.

And then he did something so extraordinary she almost dropped her mug of tea. He reached out his free hand and took hers, intertwining their fingers. "Besides, Olivia…we only have to prove our marriage is genuine, and everyone will be satisfied."

She was trembling, that much Andrew knew. Was the touch of his hand so powerful?

She asked, in a voice that shook, "What are you saying?"

"I'm saying I have no problems getting married sooner rather than later. I think we'll get along very well as husband and wife."

"Andrew…" She stopped and bit her lip. "You know we're doing this as a business arrangement. It doesn't have to go beyond that."

"But can it?"

She pulled her hand out of his and turned to stare at the falling rain. "Why would you want it to?"

Now it was his turn to be startled. "What do you mean?"

Her voice was low but firm. "Andrew, I'm not a pretty woman. I'm tall and gangly and plain. I've never been courted, for understandable reasons. In fact, I'm uncourtable. Can I be any more blunt?"

He was honestly baffled. "And you think because you feel that way, no man would ever want to court you? Including myself?"

"Well...*ja.*"

"But what if you're wrong?"

She looked at him, with an expression both bewildered and cross. "Don't tease me, Andrew. It's cruel."

"I'm not teasing." In fact, he'd never been more serious. "I'm saying I think you're wrong about being plain and uncourtable. I won't go so far as to say I love you yet, since we haven't known each other long enough to develop such feelings. But can you honestly think we'll never have any affection in this marriage of convenience?"

"I would refuse to believe they're genuine."

He was stunned at such an admission.

Helen gave a tiny grunt and fell off the bottle. Andrew tossed a dish towel over his shoulder and raised the baby to burp her. "Who hurt you?" he asked quietly.

"What do you mean?" She suddenly had a hunted look on her face.

"You say you've never been courted and, in fact, are uncourtable. You didn't come up with that by yourself. Who hurt you? What man told you that?"

"No one..."

A horrible idea came to him, one so painful that he hardly wanted to voice it. But he did. "Was it your sister?"

Olivia sprang to her feet and walked to the edge of the porch, watching the pounding rain soak the lawn. His heart nearly broke at the set of her shoulders, the rigid posture of someone trying desperately hard to control her emotions.

After a minute or two, she turned and dropped back down into the porch rocker, refusing to meet his eyes. "Maybe," she admitted.

His estimation of her sister, which was already low, now plunged into the basement. "Well, she was wrong," he said bluntly. "And I'm sorry she filled your head with such nonsense. I don't know what your sister looks like, but I'm willing to bet she fed you a pack of lies for many years solely to retain some sort of monopoly for male attention. Am I right?"

"You might be." She sniffed and fished a handkerchief out of her pocket, twisting it in her lap. "But I don't know that she was wrong.

No one has ever tried to court me. Why would they, when everyone else was prettier and more interesting? She was just telling me the truth."

He found himself infuriated with her sister. It sounded like Olivia was hurt far more deeply than even she realized. It was a cruel, hurtful thing to do to a younger sibling.

"But she wasn't telling you the truth," he contradicted. "Have you never had any man look upon you as anything other than a friend? Or were you so convinced that you weren't lovable that any interest simply didn't register?"

"I've had lots of friends who were men," she said defensively. "But it was easy to see they only saw me as a sister figure, nothing more."

"Or did your own sister convince them that's what you were?"

She had a stubborn look on her face. "You mean, did she deliberately sabotage my chances of getting married?"

"Ja."

"Maybe. And it pains me to admit it too. It paints her as an evil and horrible person, and while I have my problems with her, I don't think she's that bad. I think she's just shallow and insecure."

"Nonetheless, she hurt you. I'm going to spend the next few years trying to undo the damage she did."

She gave him a sad smile. "Is it possible?"

"*Ja*. Mere words aren't going to change your mind about how you think you look," he told her. "But I'll try. Olivia, you're not plain. Nor are you beautiful. You're nice-looking. But you have something that caught my attention from the beginning—a lovely smile, a face that lights up when you're interested or excited, beautiful eyes. Altogether, it's a powerful package, and it's one of the reasons I have no qualms about entering a marriage of convenience with you. In time, it could well be just a marriage. A regular marriage. And a happy one, I hope."

If he was expecting her to fall into his arms in profound gratitude, he was destined to be disappointed. She sniffed a bit more and applied the handkerchief to her eyes, but her expression remained controlled.

"I wish I could believe you," she said at last. "I've spent my whole life convinced I'm too ugly to be lovable, and the 'mere words,' as you say, are nice but don't seem to apply to me. As for this marriage of convenience, I can't help but feel you're getting the short end of the stick in this arrangement. After all, what happens if another woman catches your eye—a pretty one? How long before you'll regret being yoked with someone like me?"

"But you forget." He heard the tinge of bitterness creep into his tone and worked to control it. "I courted a beautiful woman. Meltingly, stunningly beautiful. And the one thing I learned is, the old cliché that beauty is only skin deep is true. Believe me, Olivia, if you were beautiful, as beautiful as you say your sister is, I would never consider any sort of partnership with you—marital, financial, anything."

She gave a rueful chuckle. "It sounds like we both have our hang-ups when it comes to beauty, then."

"I guess." He realized he was clenching Helen a bit harder than he meant to, and consciously tried to relax his muscles. "Was your father aware that your sister poisoned your mind?"

"I don't think so." She sighed. "She was always a disappointment to him because of her behavior, but I never let him know anything hurtful she did to me. He was hurt enough as it was by her antics. I know he spent endless hours praying she would return to the flock, and she never did."

"Do you think she ever will?"

"I don't know." Olivia slumped down. "I know I should pray for her, pray she'll return, but sometimes it's hard. I know I harbor a great deal of resentment, not least because she literally dumped her baby on me. How could she abandon her own child? Yet I know people have been redeemed from worse than what she's done."

"I wonder," he mused, "how much of her antagonism toward you stems from jealousy?"

"Jealous? Of me?" Olivia stared at him. "How could someone like Adele be jealous of *me*?"

"Well, consider this… What else does she have going for her besides her beauty? Because you thought you lacked it, you developed yourself into a kind and loving person, outstandingly skilled in your trade, generous enough to take a baby in, filial enough to maintain the love of your father, and surrounded by friends. What does your sister have, besides a pretty face?"

She stared out at the dripping trees and lawn. The worst of the storm had passed, and the wind had died. Only a steady patter of rain continued to softly drum on the roof overhead.

"I don't know…" she said at last. "If she is jealous, I doubt she even realizes it. But on some level, I think she's always sabotaged my confidence, perhaps to prop up her own." She shook her head. "What a sad state of affairs, *ja*?"

"*Ja*. I feel the same way about the woman I courted. She has nothing but her pretty face. When that fades, what's left?"

"Certainly not the unfading beauty of a gentle and quiet spirit," she remarked, quoting one of her favorite Bible verses.

"*Ja*, I was thinking the same thing." He smiled at her and rose from the porch rocker. "Meanwhile, this little one has fallen asleep. I'll go put her down for a nap."

Olivia stood up. "Andrew..."

He paused and looked at her. She looked almost shy. "Whatever our pasts, whatever the circumstances that brought us together, I'm glad to be here with you." The crimson returned to her cheeks.

In his head he gave a tiny fist pump of happiness. He realized he relished Olivia's good opinion and partnership. She was, in fact, growing prettier in his eyes—in part because she had that coveted unfading beauty of a gentle and quiet spirit. He realized this marriage of convenience would not be a hardship at all.

"I blame *Gott*," he said, and grinned. "From the first time I tried to figure out how to buy this farm on my own, He put the idea in my head that you might be interested in partnering with me. I never thought things would move as fast as they did. I can only see His hand in it all."

"*Ja*, me too." She seemed more relaxed now. "And tomorrow we can make it official, at least as far as owning the farm."

"We have a big day tomorrow." He gently patted Helen's back. "And a lot of our future will be decided too."

Chapter Twelve

"Sign here." The escrow officer pointed to a pair of dotted lines. Andrew signed his name, then Olivia signed hers.

"And now here. And here. And here."

It seemed like an endless series of forms, but at last their half of the paperwork for purchasing the farm was complete, and the funds from both her account and Andrew's account were transferred into the escrow account. All they needed now was the corresponding signatures from the Shrocks, which—the escrow officer told them—should be forthcoming, within a week or two. The documents would be mailed that day to the Shrocks' address in Pennsylvania.

By the time Olivia and Andrew emerged, blinking, from the title company's building into the sunny street, she felt a bit shell shocked. "I've never bought property before," she told Andrew. "It seems strange to be parting with such a large sum of money."

"Regrets?" He peered at her with some concern.

"Nein!" Her answer was definitive. "Just think what we're getting in return."

"Gut." He looked relieved. "We're one big step closer to owning the farm."

"Imagine sitting on that porch for the rest of our lives." She grinned at him. "I don't know about you, but I like the thought."

"Ja, me too." His smile was captivating. "Next stop, Yoder's Mercantile?"

"Ja."

"Helen doing okay?"

"She's probably going to need a diaper change soon, but let's see if we can hold off until after I talk to the Yoders."

Andrew directed Maggie down the town's main street until he saw Yoder's Mercantile. He guided the horse to the hitching post the Yoders had thoughtfully provided for their church customers.

Yoder's Mercantile had a large old-fashioned porch with a ramp at one end and stairs in the center. Buckets of bright flowers added splashes of color to the front of the wooden building. The window displays held colorful goods—quilts and soaps and an assortment of faceless Amish dolls and other items.

The bell tinkled overhead as Olivia pushed open the door, with Helen in the sling and Andrew trailing behind. The store had squeaky wooden floors and a huge inventory ranging from fresh fruits and vegetables, Amish crafts of all sorts, quilts, a coffee shop, soaps, and other sundries. Through a side door, Olivia knew, the Yoders ran a community cannery where people could have their garden produce professionally canned up. Some of the output of the cannery was sold in the store. They also had planned to open an in-house bakery, but Anna Miller had mentioned they couldn't find a full-time baker to hire, so the project was postponed.

But overall, the store was a catch-all establishment used as an outlet for church members to sell their goods to the *Englisch* community. It was also, she had been told, a wildly popular place for the *Englisch* townspeople to shop or linger over beverages in the coffee area.

"*Guder mariye*, Olivia, Andrew." Mabel Yoder, plump and gray haired, smiled at them.

If Olivia was concerned that Mabel was among the church people who disapproved of her living arrangements, the older woman gave no indication.

"*Guder mariye*," she replied. "I brought a selection of baskets for you to look at." She held out her prettiest pine-needle basket.

"*Ach*, it's lovely!" Mabel took the basket in hand and examined it closely.

"I have more. This is just the smallest and easiest to carry."

"Ja, gut." Mabel handed the pine-needle basket back. "Would you like Abe to help you bring them in?"

"Nein," Andrew spoke up. "I can go fetch them."

"Danke, Andrew." Olivia gave her future husband a warm smile.

"And how's this little one?" Mabel spent a few moments fussing over the baby, then redirected her attention to Olivia. "How many baskets did you bring?"

"Just one of each style, to give you an idea of what kind I make. This way you can let me know how many of what kind you're interested in carrying."

"Baskets are popular, so we may be interested in a decent selection. *Ach*, are those yours?" she exclaimed as Andrew came in with a wide sampling. "*Komm* on back to our workroom, and let's take a look."

Abe Yoder sat working on a desk in the sparsely furnished back room. He looked up and greeted both Olivia and Andrew, then exclaimed as Mabel started stacking basket samples on the desk. The older couple examined each one, chattering over the merits. Once in a while, one or the other asked a question on workmanship, but for the most part Olivia let her craft speak for itself.

Abe Yoder picked up a square basket about sixteen inches on each side. "This would be perfect to hold baskets of small fruits," he remarked idly.

Mabel's eyes widened. *"Ja!"* she exclaimed, then whirled around to face Olivia. "I don't know why I didn't think of it before! We have endless displays in the store that would look much better with baskets, and it would be a form of advertising for you as well. Are you interested in a commission for that?"

"Of course!" Olivia grinned. "Anything you need, I can make."

For the next half hour, while Andrew good-naturedly held the baby, Olivia trailed Mabel around the store, taking notes and making suggestions as to what kinds of baskets might work for various displays. She came away with a massive number of new orders on top of what she planned to sell in the store on commission.

"Whew!" she exclaimed to Andrew as they headed back out of town. She snuggled Helen in the sling, wondering how much longer the baby would behave before needing a diaper change and feeding. The infant had behaved remarkably well, and Olivia had a feeling she was on borrowed time. "I honestly never thought I'd walk away with an order that large."

"At least she's not in a hurry. I get the impression Mabel is a *gut* businesswoman—she knows when to push and when to back down as far as the client base. I know everyone in the church settlement thinks the world of the Yoders."

"That's *gut* to know. Between moving, working on my other orders and taking care of Helen, I'm going to be busy."

"And *I'm* going to start building the bins you need for your workroom today, right after we get back from talking to the bishop."

"We may need to go home first." Olivia patted Helen through the sling. "This little one has been remarkably *gut*, but I have the impression she's going to get cranky. Let's go home and get her changed and fed. Then she can sleep in the sling while we talk to the bishop."

"*Ja, gut*. Home," he added, smiling at her. "It's our home now, Olivia! Or will be, as soon as the Shrocks sign the paperwork. I still can't believe it."

"*Gott ist gut*," she replied, smiling back. "I feel so much more settled. I wasn't aware of the absence that I was feeling until now, now that it's fulfilled. This last week has certainly been an adventure!"

"It's an adventure I'm glad to be on with you," he told her sincerely. "After Sarah dumped me, I wanted to swear off women forever. I guess *Gott* had other ideas, and all I can do is run as fast as I can to keep up with where He's leading me. But I go to bed grinning at night, blessing my good fortune."

Olivia was coming to realize her soon-to-be-husband was a man of deep feelings. But she agreed with him. "If you told me two weeks ago I would be a mother, a wife and a landowner in such short order, I wouldn't have believed you."

He directed the horse up the driveway leading to the farm just as Helen started fussing. "*Gut* timing," he remarked. He pulled Maggie to a stop, and Olivia climbed down, crooning to the baby in an effort to placate her. But the baby was soon wailing.

"I'll change her if you want to prepare a bottle," Andrew offered, apparently unfazed by the howls.

"*Danke.*" She handed over the infant, and Andrew took her to the table, where a blanket and all the baby accoutrements were already laid out. She mixed the formula and watched as he stripped off the soiled garment, cleaned her skin and re-diapered her in a fresh wrapper. He sang and talked to her in a manner Olivia found charming. He was clearly going to be a good father to the sweet child.

"Ready if you are," she said, bottle in hand. She sat down in the rocking chair, and Andrew handed over the baby, who was fussing again.

She calmed down the moment the bottle hit her mouth.

"Definitely easier with two people," she concluded, nodding her thanks.

For half an hour, Helen ate her meal while Olivia and Andrew discussed the possibility of an early wedding.

"I guess we'll know within an hour or so," concluded Andrew. He rose from the chair he'd been straddling while the baby ate. "I'm going to get the horse some water before we leave. I'll swing back and pick you up."

She watched as he walked out the front door, admiring the efficient way he carried himself.

The truth was, she didn't see any reason to wait to get married. As far as she knew, Andrew hid no unpleasant surprises and hinted at no unpleasant personality quirks. He seemed just as he appeared: an honest, upright man who had been badly burned by the beautiful woman in his past.

If Andrew found no fault in her plain looks and seemed willing to accept her as a wife, and to accept Helen as his daughter, who was she to question the providence *Gott* had provided?

Thus resolved, Olivia gathered the now-sated baby, packed a few more things in the diaper basket and went out to join Andrew in trying to convince the bishop not to wait.

* * *

As the buggy approached the Beilers' home, Andrew saw Lois Beiler working in the large garden in front of the house. The older woman straightened, shaded her eyes and waved as he turned the horse into the driveway.

He directed the horse to a shady spot under a tree, then hopped out to assist Olivia from the buggy just as Lois came over to greet them.

She smiled. "*Guten tag*. This is a surprise."

"*Ja*. We had a question for the bishop. Is he home?"

"He's in his office. Let me go get him."

Lois climbed the porch steps and disappeared into the house. Trailing behind, Andrew and Olivia also climbed the steps, with Helen tucked in the sling.

"I want to talk to Lois separately," Olivia said unexpectedly in a low voice. "Are you okay talking to the bishop by yourself?"

"*Ja*, sure," he replied, startled. "But why?"

"I want to ask her, woman to woman, why she endorsed our living arrangements even at the risk of disagreeing with her own *hutband*."

He chuckled. "I'm curious about that myself. *Ja*, I'll go talk to the bishop and ask if we can get married sooner."

Lois stepped out on the porch, followed by Samuel Beiler. *"Guten tag, guten tag,"* the older man rumbled. "Would you like to come into my office?"

"Actually, Lois, may I talk with you alone?" asked Olivia with a smile.

The church leader's wife looked startled. "*Ja*, sure," she replied. "We can sit on the porch while Andrew and my husband go into his office."

Andrew nodded at Lois, then followed Samuel Beiler into the house and through a door into a sparsely furnished office. A handsome calico cat lifted her head from a basket on the desk and blinked sleepily at them.

"What is it you wanted to talk to me about?" inquired Samuel Beiler, folding himself into his chair and indicating Andrew should be seated.

Andrew scratched the cat under the chin, then sat down. "I don't know if you noticed the uncomfortable atmosphere after church yesterday, when you announced our living situation," he began. "Things were distinctly chilly."

"Are you surprised?" countered the older man. "It's not normal, and it smacks of behaviors we don't endorse. I agreed against my better judgment."

"I can assure you, we intend to keep our end of the bargain as far as separate living quarters," replied Andrew. "But it does make me wonder: Can Olivia and I get married sooner? This week or next? We would just as soon stifle any gossip."

Samuel Beiler leaned back in his chair and steepled his fingers. "I would almost think it would *encourage* gossip," he said. "People may question the urgency of the situation."

Andrew flushed. He hadn't thought of that.

"Andrew, now it's my turn to ask you something." The bishop looked serious. "I can ask since Olivia isn't here. What are your feelings for her?"

He spent a few moments gathering his thoughts. "I haven't known her for very long," he admitted, "but nothing I've seen so far makes me regret our decision to go in on the farm together, or even enter into this marriage of convenience. I have a sincere respect for her, and not a little admiration. She's a far, far cry from the woman I was courting back in Ohio. She's sweet-tempered, a hard worker and easy to talk to. To tell you the truth, Bishop Beiler, she far surpasses Sarah in everything but looks. And I learned looks can be deceiving," he added with some bitterness.

The church leader nodded. "That's *gut*, then. However, I would still counsel you to wait until November's wedding month to get married. It will give you both time to reconsider and change your minds, should you discover some sort of incompatibility. And if people are inclined to gossip about your living arrangements…well, that's on you. You'll have to squash the gossip one person at a time."

"I see." He was a little annoyed at the bishop's inflexibility but not inclined to argue. He knew he and Olivia were already walking on shaky ground, and he didn't want to push the issue. Instead, he tried a different tact. "Olivia and I both wonder if we're suffering from the sin of coveting. Both of us felt strongly—and independently—that we belonged on the farm, that *Gott* had provided the perfect place for us to live. Is that coveting? Are we wrong for wanting the farm so badly?"

"Coveting is complex," replied the bishop. "And while I understand you and Olivia are both doing unusual things to obtain the farm, you're not resorting to theft or violence or other sinful activities to obtain it. What you're sacrificing, apparently, is your reputations."

"Even though we're not living together." It was a statement, not a question.

"Even so," agreed the bishop. "Coveting is wanting something at someone else's expense. Aside from the money you're both contributing toward purchasing the farm, the only other expense you're paying is the reputation you're developing in the process—and that's something you'll both just have to deal with."

"Bishop, I respectfully urge you to consider letting us get married right away," Andrew said quietly. "May I ask you to pray on it? Both Olivia and I are anxious not to jeopardize our standing in the church. An early private wedding would allay those concerns. We could have a public church wedding in November, as we originally planned, as well."

Bishop Beiler eyed him silently for a few moments. The cat rested her head back on her paws. The animal's movements caught the church leader's eyes and seemed to trigger a change in him.

"There was one time," he said slowly, his eyes on the cat, "when I stubbornly wouldn't budge from a position I held about a member of our church. Then this person did something that changed my mind entirely and made me realize how wrong I had been. I realized that the sin of *hochmut*—pride—can even affect church leaders." He shifted his gaze and met Andrew's eyes. "It was not a situation I care to repeat. If you feel you and Olivia are being called by *Gott* to marry this early, then I will pray on it and let you know my answer tomorrow."

Andrew's hopes soared, but he kept his expression grave. "*Danke*, Bishop Beiler. Shall we stop by tomorrow for your answer?"

"*Ja*, that would be fine." The bishop looked stern. "I have not yet given my approval," he warned. "Don't make assumptions. But I will try to listen to what *Gott* is telling me."

Andrew nodded. "I appreciate your consideration. Olivia and I will swing by tomorrow about this time. *Vielen dank*, Bishop." He rose and touched the brim of his hat, then walked out of the office.

On the front porch, he saw Lois and Olivia in deep discussion, and both seemed startled at his sudden appearance.

"Oh!" exclaimed Olivia, and blushed.

Blushed? What were she and Lois discussing?

"Ready to go?" he asked.

"Um, *ja*. *Ja*, sure." She rose from the porch rocker with Helen still tucked snugly in the sling. She nodded to Lois. *"Danke,"* she added.

The older woman nodded and smiled, and it seemed to Andrew she had a twinkle in her eyes. *"Bitte,"* she replied simply.

He didn't say much as he walked with Olivia back to the buggy. After assisting her in, he took the driver's seat, picked up the reins and clucked to Maggie.

"The bishop hasn't given us a definitive answer about getting married right away," he said bluntly.

She wilted. "Really?"

"Really. When I mentioned the cold shoulders we'd gotten after church yesterday, he essentially said 'I told you so' without actually saying 'I told you so.' But he did say, effectively, that we've made our beds and must lie in them."

"Wunnerschee," she said sarcastically.

"That's what I thought. When I argued that getting married right away would stifle any gossip, he said it might encourage gossip instead since people may...may question the urgency of the situation."

She gasped and spread a hand across her chest. "That never occurred to me."

"Nein, me either. But while we were talking, the oddest thing happened. He has a cat that was sleeping in a basket on his desk. The cat made a movement that caught his eye. He stared at the cat and said he was once afflicted with *hochmut* when it came to some issue with a church member, and he had to learn to put his pride aside. Then he said he would pray on the issue of whether to marry us sooner, and he'll give us an answer tomorrow."

"Tomorrow?" she parroted. "So we need to come back tomorrow?"

"Ja."

She blew out a breath. "That actually sounds more hopeful."

"He warned me not to get my hopes up," Andrew said. Holding the reins one-handed, he removed his hat and ran a hand through his hair in a gesture of frustration. "Honestly, Olivia, I don't see a need to wait, but it's not my call. Without the bishop's blessing, we can't change our plans."

"Then we must also pray," she said, and sighed. "I know it's not easy putting up with gossip and rumors in what is, after all, a new community for both of us—but the bishop is going to have to back us up. We've been completely open and transparent about our plans and our motivation. It's not like we can be shunned for doing something he approved of, however reluctantly."

"It's just annoying, I suppose." He slumped down. "All my life, I've considered myself an upstanding member of the church. This is the first time it's been questioned."

"Maybe that's the price we're both paying for coveting the farm so much."

"Ah. Coveting. Actually, I brought that up to the bishop. He explained that coveting is wanting something at someone else's expense. Since that's not what we're doing with the farm—since we've harmed no one and we've paid for it honestly—then we're not coveting...especially since the only harm, if you can call it that, is to our reputations."

"Well, that's *gut*, I suppose." She gazed out at the passing landscape, absently patting the sleeping baby on the back. "Hopefully, he'll change his mind so we won't have to endure the cold shoulders until November."

"At which point, presumably, people will understand there was no 'urgency' to our situation."

She chuckled. *"Ja."*

He admired her in that moment. Despite the uncertainty in their plans, she took everything in stride. How different Olivia was from Sarah.

"But, Olivia..." He paused. "I want you to know that should the bishop consent to marry us, I will consider it little more than a binding agreement. Nothing will change in my living situation until after our proper wedding in November, and even then, I'm willing to follow your lead on what makes you comfortable."

He saw hot color rise in her cheeks. *"Danke,* Andrew."

Long after they had returned home and went about their separate tasks for the rest of the afternoon and evening, he thought about the contrast between the two women, Sarah and Olivia. They were as different as night from day. And where once he would have seen nothing but sunshine in Sarah, now he thought about her in unpleasant shades of darkness.

By contrast, despite her less harmonious features, Olivia brought sunshine wherever she went. He found himself looking forward to basking in those rays of warmth, both in the short term and in the long run.

It wasn't until much later, when he was just

starting to drift off to sleep in the small guest cabin, that he realized he'd forgotten to ask Olivia what she and Lois had been discussing so intently while he had been talking with the bishop.

Chapter Thirteen

The next afternoon, Olivia interrupted her work of putting the house in order to change into a fresh apron before going to the bishop's. After all, it was conceivable she could be a married woman by this afternoon.

When she climbed into the buggy next to Andrew, it seemed he had changed his shirt and washed his face for the same reason. But he said nothing about it, and neither did she.

"I'm nervous," she admitted as Andrew clucked to the horse and they started for the bishop's home. She held the baby in the sling and watched the passing scenery. "If the bishop's answer is still *nein*, then I'll make plans to move out until November. But I don't want to. With all the basket orders Mabel just gave me, it would be difficult to fill those orders *and* care for a baby without your help."

"Just as I don't relish living at the farm by myself," he replied. He kept his eyes on the road.

"It's a place made for a family, and just the brief taste of what it's like to live there with you and Helen makes me want more. But no matter what comes, we'll make it work."

That was one of the things she admired about Andrew. He made things work.

Within a few minutes, they approached the bishop's small farm. Discreetly, Olivia wiped her damp palms on her apron as Andrew drew up the horse under the shade of a tree and climbed out of the buggy.

Lois Beiler emerged onto the front porch. *"Guten tag,"* she greeted, smiling.

Olivia, looking at Lois's welcoming face, couldn't detect whether she would leave their home as a married woman or not. *"Guten tag,"* she replied cautiously.

"*Komm* in, *komm* in." Lois held open the screen door invitingly.

Olivia passed through, followed by Andrew, just as Bishop Beiler came out of his office. He offered them both a thin smile. *"Guten tag,"* he greeted. "Are you ready to get married?"

Olivia's whole world shifted. Suddenly, everything seemed glorious. *"Ja, bitte!"* she exclaimed. She glanced at Andrew and saw he was looking at the church leader with an enormous smile on his face.

"Danke, Bishop!" he said enthusiastically.

The church leader chuckled, then sobered. "I can't say I still don't have reservations," he cautioned. "But I've prayed on it and talked it over with Lois, and I'm willing to proceed."

"You won't regret it," Andrew assured him. "We get along well, Bishop Beiler, and I can't help but feel *Gott* is leading us to make this commitment."

"Very well."

The brief wedding ceremony hardly fazed Olivia at all. She had been to dozens of weddings, and without the attendance of church witnesses, it almost seemed like play-acting. Yet she knew the vows were serious.

Lois Beiler held the baby. Andrew took Olivia's hand and repeated the ancient vows. *This is it*, she thought. But she wasn't nervous—she was confident. She remembered Andrew's words from last night: this would not change their living situation. In her opinion, they were still business partners, little more.

In the end, Andrew turned and kissed her—a quick and passionless one that nonetheless left her reeling. She felt color rise in her cheeks and her heart started pounding.

"Congratulations!" Lois Beiler smiled warmly at them both. "May *Gott* bless your marriage."

"Danke!" Olivia and Andrew said together. She glanced at him just as he glanced at her, and they both burst out laughing.

"Laughter is a *gut* sign," admitted the bishop, who unthawed enough to smile. "Now, Lois has a small treat for you in the kitchen."

The treat turned out to be a small wedding cake, elaborately frosted, with a side of freshly made peach ice cream. Olivia was deeply touched. *"Vielen dank!"* she exclaimed. "You didn't have to do this, Lois!"

"My hope is, you'll have a proper wedding in November," said Lois. She cut the cake and scooped up ice cream, gesturing for everyone to sit at the kitchen table.

In that moment, Olivia realized how much she valued the bishop and his wife. Despite their misgivings, they were willing to give her and Andrew a solid chance at happiness. She promised herself not to let them down.

Later, on the buggy ride back to their new home, Olivia hugged Helen to her chest and said as much to Andrew. "I know they—or at least the bishop—were reluctant to let us follow through, but they did. Lois even made us cake and ice cream. I found myself mentally promising not to let them down."

"You too?" He took his eyes off the road and glanced at her. "I found myself thinking much the same thing. We both have strong motivations, Olivia. We'll make this work."

* * *

Olivia didn't think she'd ever been as happy, or as productive, as those first few weeks spent with Andrew on the farm.

Andrew kept his word in every regard. He spent the first full week outfitting her studio exactly to her every wish, and Olivia gloried in the efficient setup that allowed her to keep all her basket-making supplies in good order. In fact, she spent a full day not doing any more work than just filling every bin and every box he supplied, and smiling with pleasure the whole time. It took all her willpower not to hug Andrew with sheer gratitude for his hard work. She still felt shy about her growing attraction to the man.

She made it up through praise. "It's perfect," she told him, standing in the center of the room, Helen in her arms. She spun in a slow circle. "See, I've got all the weaving supplies there. And I've collected the needles, twine, string and other sewing supplies over here. And you're right, a shipping station was a *gut* idea. Look, it even holds the largest flattened boxes I could ever need!" She hugged the baby in sheer excitement.

Andrew chuckled and ran his thumbs through his suspenders. "Once upon a time, I thought about making something similar for Sarah, a dedicated workspace for her. She was a talented quilter. But she never would have admitted any pleasure in anything I could do for her. I'd far rather do things for *you*."

She met his eyes, crinkled at the corners from smiling, and turned away shyly. This business arrangement was becoming far more personal—at least to her—than she'd ever anticipated.

"Well, it's *wunnerschee*," she reiterated. "I can't even begin to tell you how grateful I am."

"Now, let's figure out your work schedule," he suggested. "What time of day do you prefer to work? Morning, noon, night? I'm flexible."

"Morning and afternoon," she replied. "Back with *Daed*, my typical day was to work for a couple hours in the morning, break for lunch, then a couple hours in the afternoon. If I try to work much longer than that, my back gets tired from bending over."

He nodded. "That would fit in well with what I hope to accomplish on the farm. I can get the chores done early, maybe start a project, then take over watching Helen while you get your work done and repeat that in the afternoon."

Again, she felt profound gratitude toward the man. He was being so generous with his time.

And it worked. Over the next few weeks, they developed a superb working schedule that allowed both of them to lavish attention on Helen while getting their respective work finished.

"She's growing," he remarked one day early in September, gently playing with Helen's feet as the baby looked around alertly from her bouncer seat in the middle of the kitchen table. "She's going to be sitting up soon."

"*Ja*. And what a beautiful baby she is." Olivia tickled the infant under the chin. The baby had started babbling nonsense sounds. "She looks remarkably like my sister. I just hope she doesn't decide to *act* like my sister."

"Well, we'll both work to raise her up in the faith." Andrew took a bite of the hearty stew Olivia had made for lunch. "At least things have eased with the rest of the church community. I guess everyone figured out we just took an unusual method to purchase this farm and there were no 'urgent circumstances' around our actions."

"I suspect the bishop and Lois have been instrumental in quashing any rumors," Olivia remarked.

"That reminds me…" Andrew put down his spoon and reached for some corn bread. "I always meant to ask what it was you and Lois were discussing that day on the porch, when I was inside talking to the bishop."

"Oh!" Olivia felt her cheeks grow hot. "Well, ah, I don't know if I can talk about it. It was, um, kind of a woman-to-woman conversation."

"I see." Andrew gave a sort of half smile. She could tell he was curious but wouldn't pursue it. Olivia admired him for his restraint.

The truth was, she had asked Lois why the older woman had seen to champion their unorthodox approach to marriage and buying the farm, even in the face of her husband's disapproval. Lois's reply had astounded Olivia.

"Because I can see he's the right man for you," Lois had said. "And the fact that *Gott* is opening every door makes me think this is His will for you. It may come at a cost, but nothing in life is easy."

"I can't help but feel I'm unlovable," she had confessed. "I'm so plain, you see."

Lois had shaken her head. "Put aside the idea that men are only attracted to beauty," she advised. "Of course it's easy to only see the externals at first. That's human nature. But it's what's inside that counts. Many times, a beautiful woman is beautiful inside as well as outside. But when she's not, no amount of outside beauty can compensate for that inner ugliness. You're a lot prettier than you seem to think, but however you see yourself, it's obvious Andrew sees deeper. Let *Gott* lead you to whatever your future holds."

"But if we do get married, what happens if he meets a woman who's better looking than I am?"

"You're both young. You have years ahead of you to meet people who are better looking than either of you," Lois replied. "So you look at them as a piece of artwork, admire them for a moment, then turn to the spouse you married and let them know how much you love them. Under no circumstances do either of you act on a temporary attraction."

"*Ja*, I think that's my sister's weakness," she admitted.

Lois had given her other womanly advice, and Olivia had held the older woman's words close to her heart and treasured them. She also knew this wasn't anything she could discuss with Andrew…at least, not yet.

And now here was Andrew, almost two months into this strange business arrangement they had cobbled together, and he had proven himself to be everything she could want in a *hutband*.

How he felt about her personally was a bit more enigmatic.

But he was companionable, pleasant, hardworking and true to his word. Olivia blessed *Gott* for bringing him to her doorstep that one evening to propose co-purchasing the farm. Beyond that…she was willing to take Lois's advice and let *Gott* lead her to whatever her future held.

In another six or seven weeks, they would be getting married properly, with church witnesses. At that point, Andrew would move into the house from the little outside shed where he'd been sleeping. Whether he would occupy a separate bedroom was something Olivia didn't know...though she wondered.

But one thing was certain: Helen was thriving under both their care. "I wonder what happened in her early life," Olivia mused, playing with the baby's hand and feeling the little fingers curl in a tight grip around her much larger finger. "This little creature is so darling I don't think I could ever give her up. I wonder if Adele ever regrets her actions."

"Have you heard from her?"

"Nein." Olivia shook her head. "But that's nothing unusual. I expect she'll show up on my doorstep one day. That's been her habit for the last ten years—she dips back into my life whenever she needs to decompress and recover from her latest love affair. Then she's off again. She's thirty-three. I wonder how much longer she thinks she can keep acting like a youngie and never settle down."

"Well, in a weird way, I'm glad we have Helen. I feel like she's mine." Andrew smiled at the baby. "I've always wanted *kinner*, and I think that's one of the reasons I was so bitter after Sarah left me. It's like she took my future *bopplin* away. But now I have Helen."

Olivia's heart swelled.

Lest she become overwhelmed with emotion, she changed the subject. "I've got the rest of the Yoders' display baskets finished, and I also have a shipment to send out. I think I'll hitch up Maggie and take a trip into town this afternoon and get everything delivered. I'll take the *boppli*," she added, "so you can get some work done."

"Ja, gut," he replied. "I want to finish harvesting the carrots and potatoes from the garden. I have a feeling we're going to see our first frost in a week or so. It's time to get things under cover."

And so it continues, Olivia thought later, as she slipped the bit in Maggie's mouth and hitched the horse to the buggy. They acted, in all ways, as a married couple, with one enormous exception. But they were getting to know each other and discovering how compatible they were.

For herself, she had no desire to separate. In fact, she looked forward to getting married properly…whether it was a business arrangement or something more.

With Helen in a sturdy basket on the seat beside her, she trotted the horse toward town and thanked *Gott* that He had seen to provide her with everything she wanted. Not only did she have a way to earn a living through her craft, but He had sent her a child to raise and a *hutband* to be her helpmate. As for the farm—well, she never regretted spending her money to buy half of it. It was a magnificent setting in which to live, and she was grateful for the privilege.

Yet there *was* something more she wanted. More and more in the last few weeks, her thoughts had come to dwell on Andrew. Would he ever be healed from the injury his betrothed had inflicted on him? She didn't know.

But should that day come, she hoped it would be her—Plain Olivia—who could provide the bandage for the wound.

Andrew watched Olivia drive the buggy away with a smile on his face. She was an amazingly competent woman. She had hitched up the horse and driven away as if doing so was an everyday occurrence, though he knew many Amish women never drove on their own.

But if she had been caring for her childhood farm during her father's illness, he supposed it made sense. There was very little Olivia couldn't do once she set her mind to something.

He picked up several sturdy baskets she had made for garden use and went out the back door to the large vegetable patch fenced against the deer. The potatoes were ready to harvest, as were the onions, carrots, cayenne peppers and dried beans. The tomatoes were still largely green—he was told by other gardeners that the area's shorter summers meant tomatoes were often harvested green and allowed to ripen indoors during autumn. With a frost coming on, he decided to harvest every tomato he could, ripe or not.

All in all, he was a happy man as he bent his back to his afternoon's work.

Two hours later, with baskets overflowing with harvested vegetables, he straightened up and peered at the position of the sun in the sky. Olivia should be home soon, and Helen with her. Impulsively he scooped up some late-season wildflowers and laid them on top of one of the baskets of produce, which he then heaved up and brought to the back porch.

When all the vegetables were brought in, he brought the bouquet of tansy and asters into the kitchen and plopped them in a quart jar of water. He had just placed the jar in the center of the kitchen table when he was startled by a knock at the front door.

They seldom had visitors, so the knock was both unexpected and a bit concerning. Was a neighbor in trouble? Did the bishop wish to talk with him?

But when he opened the door, he saw a woman about his age dressed in *Englisch* clothing of a casual blouse over a skirt that ended just above her knees. She was stunningly beautiful and gave him a melting smile. To his astonishment, she spoke in German.

"I'm looking for Olivia Bontrager," she said. "Does she live here?"

"Ja," he replied. "But she's not home right now." He paused. "And who are you?"

"I'm Adele Bontrager," she replied. "I'm her sister."

Andrew felt almost like the floor was opening up beneath him. Olivia hadn't exaggerated when she'd described her sister as beautiful. She had dark, almost black, hair, chocolate-brown eyes, a smile that could knock a man flat at ten paces and the poised confidence of someone who knows she's stunning.

He blithered. "She—she took the b-buggy into town. I expect her back any moment."

"And you are…?"

"Andrew Eicher." He paused. Trying to explain the complexity of his association with Olivia seemed futile at the moment. Getting a hold of himself, he said, "May I offer you some lemonade?"

"Ja, danke." She made a motion as if to walk into the house, but Andrew knew it would be a mistake to be alone indoors with this woman.

Instead, he gestured firmly toward the porch rockers. "If you'll have a seat, I'll bring it out."

She gave him that incredible smile again, as if guessing his extremely visceral reaction, and demurely seated herself in one of the rockers.

Andrew closed the door behind him and spent a moment or two composing himself. It was an instinctive and joltingly masculine reaction to utter feminine beauty, and he was furious with himself for his response.

He poured lemonade into two glasses with hands that shook a bit, then brought them out to the porch. He seated himself across the small table from her. "I'm surprised to see you here."

"So you've heard of me?"

"Ja."

"And how do you know my sister?"

He kept his explanation brief. "She's my business partner. We co-own this farm."

"Really?" Her eyebrows rose. "Do you both live here?"

"Ja. But in separate residences," he hastened to add. Trying to explain the complexities of their marriage of convenience seemed futile at the moment.

"And…" For a moment, Adele's voice trembled. "And does Olivia have my baby?"

"Ja," he replied in a gentler tone. Maybe she was regretting abandoning Helen? "They've grown inseparable."

"Ahh…"

Adele was silent a moment, looking out past the Virginia creeper—just starting to turn color—and toward the buffer of trees that hemmed in the farm. He took the opportunity to study her features. Except for the tiniest of wrinkles at the corners of her eyes, she could pass for someone ten years younger. Her nose was perfect, her cheekbones high, her stunning dark hair was in a single long braid down her back.

No wonder Olivia doubted her own looks, growing up in the shadow of such a sister.

She turned and caught him examining her, and he instantly averted his gaze. To his annoyance, he felt heat in his cheeks.

"I hope Olivia isn't too annoyed by what I did," said Adele. Her tone managed to convey that she was fully aware of his response to her appearance but was skilled in deflecting the attention.

"You threw her for a loop," he said bluntly. "It was a rotten thing to do, to abandon your own child."

"Is that what you think I did?" Her laugh sounded like silver bells. "I didn't *abandon* Helen. I merely thought her aunt might like to get to know her."

It was as blatant a lie as he'd ever heard, and in that instant, Andrew snapped to his senses. All Adele's beauty suddenly turned ugly in his eyes. What good was physical perfection if the heart was shriveled and dried up?

Like a lance to his side, he remembered Sarah's callous abandonment. While his old betrothed and Olivia's sister were very different in looks, each was uncannily beautiful in her own right. And yet the momentary blindness he experienced upon meeting Adele was stripped away when he recalled Sarah's betrayal.

Was beauty synonymous with shallowness? He couldn't imagine it was—he knew many beautiful women were both kind and goodhearted—but why was it the two most beautiful women he'd ever seen were both heartless?

But he kept a lock on his tongue. Like it or not, this woman was his sister-in-law. He kept his tone polite and conversational. "How was Europe?"

"*Ach*, it was wonderful! We saw so many things—Venice and Paris and Amsterdam and London…"

Evidently it was a good question, for Andrew was able to stay quiet and just listen to Adele chatter about the various exotic sights she'd seen. And in the back of his mind was a longing for Olivia to show up—not just to rescue him from Adele's company, but also because somehow, she seemed purer and more refined than her sister.

In fact, envisioning Olivia's face before him, he realized how much he treasured her. The smile that lit up her plain features, her eyes that could twinkle with humor, the stunning brown hair that—braided—reached well past her waist on the rare times he'd seen it down. And most of all, he treasured her kindness and peaceful nature.

Instinct told him that any time spent in Adele's company was unlikely to be peaceful.

"So, what is it you do?"

Andrew came out of his reverie to see Adele's eyes fixed on him with flattering attention.

"I'm a farmer," he replied shortly. "What do you think?"

"I think you're a *gut* Amish man," she replied. "Salt of the earth. Clever at making and fixing things. At home with a hammer in his hands. An expert with horses and cattle. Am I right?"

"You grew up Amish," he retorted mildly. "You just described ninety percent of Amish men." He didn't like the slightly flirtatious tone she was adopting, and he prayed Olivia would return soon. He turned the tables. "And what is it *you* do?"

"Me?" Again came her silvery laugh. "I just flit around the world, drinking in wonderful sights, living off the fat of the land."

"Sounds expensive."

"Depends on how you go about doing it." Her smile was definitely flirtatious.

"And what are you doing here?"

"Why, visiting my sister, of course. And seeing my baby."

"How long are you staying?"

He almost missed the flicker of uncertainty that passed over her features before she composed herself. "That depends."

"On what?"

"Oh…" She fluttered her hand and then fluttered her eyelashes. "Lots of things. Now, stop interrogating me and tell me what's happening with my baby."

It was with profound gratitude that Andrew heard the distinct clip-clop of Maggie's hooves coming up the driveway through the tunnel of trees.

"There's Olivia," he announced, rising from his porch rocker. "Why don't you stay here, and I'll let her know you've arrived."

"Sure thing, *liebling.*"

The endearment was jarring. Andrew turned his back on Adele, descended the porch steps and strode across the lawn.

Seeing him, Olivia smiled and pulled the horse up. "All finished delivering baskets!" she said happily. "And Mabel Yoder said they've nearly sold out of the baskets I brought in two weeks ago and wants another order."

"That's *gut.*" Andrew walked up to the buggy on the passenger side, where Helen rested in her special travel basket Olivia had made. "Olivia…" He met her eyes. "We have a visitor."

At the gravity in his voice, the joy drained from Olivia's face, and she looked toward the house. She went pale.

"Adele."

"*Ja.*"

She lifted her chin and straightened her shoulders as if bracing to do battle. "I suppose I knew this day would come," she said quietly.

"I'll take care of the horse and buggy," he offered. "And do you want me to take Helen as well?"

"*Nein*, I'll take her. After all…" She gave a mirthless laugh. "No doubt the doting mother can't wait to see the daughter she abandoned."

He heard the jangle of bitterness in her voice and couldn't blame her.

Chapter Fourteen

Olivia climbed down from the buggy and lifted Helen from the basket. Andrew met her eyes, grave and questioning, before taking the horse by the bridle and leading her toward the barn.

She hitched the baby over her shoulder, took a deep breath and then turned toward the house.

Adele sat in the porch rocker, clasping a glass of lemonade, a half smile on her face. Olivia couldn't decide if her expression was smug or apologetic. *Likely both*, she thought.

"I'm surprised to see you here," Olivia said.

Adele smiled. "You led me on a merry chase, little sister. I had to ask all over the place to find out where you were."

"Why did you bother?"

"Isn't it obvious? I wanted to see my baby."

"*Your* baby? Don't you mean *my* baby?" Olivia clasped Helen more firmly.

"Says the woman who never got married. Come on, let me have her."

Olivia mounted the porch steps and, without much resistance, laid the infant in her sister's arms.

"Ahh..." Adele smiled at Helen and made kitchy-coo noises. "She's grown!"

"Of course she's grown. You've been gone almost three months."

Helen stared at her mother in confusion, making no effort to smile. Olivia took some satisfaction in that, since Helen smiled readily at both her and Andrew now.

"So, who's the stud?" Adele gave Olivia a wicked smile and jerked her head in the direction Andrew had gone.

Trying to explain her complex living situation seemed futile. Besides, her sister's taunts from years back about being "uncourtable" still stung. She didn't want her association with Andrew to be contaminated by Adele's derision. Olivia fell back upon the brief explanation she and Andrew had devised long ago. "He's my business partner. We co-own this farm."

"Those are almost precisely the same words he used. Does this mean you're living together?" Adele tipped her head back and let loose a belly laugh. "Oh, that's rich!" The baby, startled by the whoop of mirth, screwed up her face as if getting ready to cry.

"We are *not* living together," Olivia spat furiously. "What part of 'business partner' don't you understand?"

"How can you both own this farm and not be living together?" The wicked glint remained in her sister's eyes.

Olivia was by no means pleased that Adele had so quickly pinpointed the theological uncertainty of the situation. She decided to forestall mentioning that she and Andrew had already had a private ceremony that, technically, united them. From past experience, she knew her sister would simply use that bit of information as a weapon.

"He stays in another building," she said. "The only way he could afford this property is if we both pitched in for the purchase price. In exchange, he helps care for Helen."

"How convenient," Adele replied, with just a hint of a sneer in her tone.

"Don't interpret my situation through the lens of your own experience," snapped Olivia. "Now, let me have Helen back. She doesn't know you anymore."

"I'm considering taking Helen with me," mused Adele, looking with intent at the baby in her arms.

Olivia stiffened. A shiver of horror ran through her. "You'll do nothing of the sort. You abandoned her. She's mine now."

"Is that so?" Adele leaned back on the rocker with an air of insolence. "I thought you were just caretaking her for me while I was in Europe."

"If you try to take Helen back, I will take you to court." Olivia spoke with dead-serious conviction. "You've been here only a few minutes and have done little except lob insults, even though I'm the one who took in your baby when you abandoned her. Remember, I still have the note you put in the suitcase when you dropped her off and fled without even checking whether I was home. Nor do you have a stable home life. No judge in his right mind would award you custody." She glanced over as Andrew emerged from the barn, heading for the porch.

"We'll see about that." Following her gaze, Adele homed in on Andrew walking toward them. Like a switch had been flipped, she put on what Olivia had always thought of as her "man face"—a sultry expression designed to charm the opposite sex. "What do you say, Andrew?" she said with a pout as Andrew ascended the porch steps. "Olivia says I shouldn't be able to keep my own child." Her arms tightened around the baby.

"Do you want her back?" he asked in a surprised tone. He leaned against a porch post.

"Why wouldn't I want my own baby?" She looked at Helen and, in Olivia's mind, positively simpered.

"Perhaps she *should* be with her mother..." Andrew said slowly.

Unable to believe her own ears, Olivia whirled on him. "*Nein!* That is out of the question. You don't know my sister as I do. She'll neglect Helen while she's off pursuing her own selfish pleasures. The baby is far better off with me. I can give her stability."

Underneath her defense of the baby, Olivia was conscious of dismay. The fact that Andrew could even suggest returning the infant to her sister meant he, too, was falling under the spell of Adele's beauty. Olivia might be able to keep her niece, but would she be able to keep the man she was technically married to?

"Listen to her." Adele bounced the baby gently on her knee. "Has she ever been a mother? Now, enough of this. Tell me about the farm, Andrew. Do I understand you both put money in to buy it?"

"*Ja,*" Andrew replied. "That's what I told you earlier. I'm sure Olivia told you about our financial arrangement?"

"It seems very...cozy," Adele observed.

Olivia stiffened at the implication. She glanced at Andrew and saw, to her distress, that he wasn't disgusted with her sister's attitude as she was. Instead, he had the expression of a typical interested male.

A little part of her died inside.

Could Andrew not see through Adele's obvious facade? For decades, her sister had cultivated an innate coquetry until it was honed like a weapon. Olivia had long ago learned that no man would look at her when her sister was present. Now it seemed even Andrew had fallen under Adele's spell.

Adele spoke with animation, holding Helen like a doll, her entire attention focused on flattering Andrew, seeming to hang on to every word he said.

Mentally, Olivia wrapped herself in a familiar cloak of misery. She was tied to Andrew through half ownership of the farm. It also seemed that the bishop's concerns about marrying a man she barely knew were coming to pass, as her beautiful sister dominated his attention. Not for the first time, Olivia lamented the contrast in loveliness between her and her sibling.

"Well." Andrew boosted himself away from the porch post. "I'll let you two sisters visit. I need to do the barn chores."

"Ooh, take me along," said Adele eagerly. "It's been a long time since I've been on a farm. I wouldn't mind seeing everything!"

"Well…okay." Andrew seemed surprised by her eagerness, but he didn't argue.

Adele shoved Helen back at Olivia, tucked

her hand into the crook of Andrew's arm and descended the porch steps with him, chattering the whole time.

Olivia was so startled by the abruptness of her sister's actions that she hardly knew how to respond. Helen screwed up her little face as if equally confused by the sudden change in personnel.

Watching the pair of them walking toward the barn while she stayed behind with the baby somehow seemed symbolic. It also twisted a knife in her heart, because she realized Adele was walking away with the man she loved. That realization brought more pain than she wanted to admit.

Olivia looked at the face of her little baby and knew what she had to do. Even if Andrew chose Adele over herself, she still had her dignity... and her niece.

One thing was certain: she had no intention of hanging around to watch her sister ensnare the man who was, technically, her husband. She went into the cabin and packed a basket with baby things and a change of clothes and some toiletries for herself. She tucked Helen into the sling, took the handle of the basket and left the house.

It was a bit of a walk to her old rental cabin, but she knew it was still empty and never locked. She didn't look toward the barn, but instead followed the driveway through the tunnel of trees, then turned onto the road.

The distance was tiring, carrying both a baby and a basket, but it proved to be an excellent time for a good hard talk with herself. She wasn't about to give up Helen to her wastrel sister. That much was certain. But it was hard—very hard—to realize Andrew was no different than other men when it came to responding to Adele's obvious allure.

Olivia could not compete with her sister. She had no intention of trying. It was just the latest of a long line of bitter pills she'd been forced to swallow throughout her life, knowing Adele simply had to crook her little finger and men would come running.

But this time it was worse. This time Adele was deliberately stealing her man.

She'd fooled herself into believing Andrew's story about not being attracted to beautiful women after his fiancée's desertion. But when push came to shove, it was a tale as old as time. Beauty won. *Again.*

Unfortunately, this revelation came too late, and now she was bound to Andrew irrevocably. But nothing said they had to live together. She was perfectly capable of earning a living through her own skills. And if she had fallen into a comfortable routine with Andrew when it came to divvying up childcare so she could get work done…well, she would just stay up late and work through the night to fill her basket orders.

As for the farm…it was wrenching to give it up, but she would settle with Andrew later. At the moment, she needed to escape.

Bitterly, she wished she had listened to the bishop's advice about postponing the wedding. Regret plagued her now that Andrew had met Adele.

It was these hard, harsh thoughts that sustained her on the walk through the dusk back to the rental cabin, the precious bundle of Helen's little body snug against hers. And if she had to dash away a few tears along the way, she was only human.

Andrew's whole purpose in choosing that particular time to do barn chores was to escape Adele's cloying presence. He wasn't pleased when she shoved the baby back at Olivia, tucked her hand in the crook of his arm and escorted him to the barn.

But he was bred for politeness. Like it or not, this woman was his sister-in-law. No sense in making Olivia's family situation any more complicated by alienating her only sibling.

"How many animals do you have?" asked Adele.

"Two cow-calf pairs and three horses," he replied. "Two draft horses and our buggy horse." On the pretext of picking up a pitchfork, he was able to disentangle his arm from her grip.

She followed him closely through the shadowed interior of the barn, where he made himself busy by mucking out pens and adding fresh straw to the horse and cow stalls. He shooed the calves into the calf box, then tied up one of the cows in the milking stall. Straddling the milking stool, he milked out first one cow, then the other, pouring the milk into a sterilized tank. If he had hoped these tasks would daunt Adele, he was wrong.

Despite her veneer of sophistication, she revealed her rural upbringing by peppering him with questions about the quantity and quality of milk he got, properly identified the cows as Jerseys and inquired about plowing techniques with the draft horses. How much grass hay did the property yield? How many bushels of wheat?

"I don't know," he said, exasperated by her questions. "Keep in mind we've only been in possession of the farm for a couple months. The grass hay was harvested before we moved in, and I haven't yet harvested the wheat, so I don't know what the yield will be."

"And what farm products do you hope to sell in town?"

And so the questions continued. It wasn't that Andrew had no interest in discussing the intricacies of his new property; he was self-conscious about being alone with a woman who was a virtual stranger.

He'd been alone with women before, so why was he so anxious to escape? It took him a few minutes to realize why Adele made him uncomfortable. In a low-key but constant way, she was flirting.

He doubted she was even aware of it. It seemed innate and unconscious. It also seemed completely artificial. What was she really, truly like, he wondered?. Her entire personality seemed built on pretense. How could such a woman have sprung from the same parents as Olivia?

And despite—or because of—the dramatic difference in appearance between the two sisters, he found himself far preferring Olivia's honest purity. He enjoyed how her face lit up when she smiled, the sparkle of humor and affection in her blue eyes, and her complete lack of artifice.

And so he grew increasingly irked by Adele's presence and her inherent assumption that her beauty should trump any other qualities. Her chatter became annoying and her presence cloying.

"…tonight," she was saying.

"I'm sorry, what?" He'd already tuned her out. "I missed the question."

"I said, I'm hoping you have a place where I can sleep tonight."

For one horrified moment, he thought she was actually propositioning him before his common sense rejected the thought. "You'll have to talk to Olivia," he answered, moving toward a stall to let a cow inside. "She might be able to find room for you."

Adele pouted. "She's always short-tempered with me. I was hoping you could give me a definite answer."

"Well, I can't. Olivia is in charge of the house—" it wasn't true, but Adele didn't know that "—and she'll have to give you a final answer."

"If you say so." To his shock, she ran a hand up his arm.

Instinctively, he knocked her hand off and whirled around to face her. "Adele, stop it. You're a stranger to me, and that's not appropriate behavior."

"I don't have to be a stranger." She pouted at him, looking adorably pretty.

But all Andrew could see was Sarah and her exotic beauty. His former fiancée looked nothing like Adele, but they had similar qualities of sensuality that disturbed him. Sarah had played him like a violin, capitalizing on her looks while concealing the cold heart that lay within. He couldn't see Adele being any different.

"I need to take care of the chickens," he

blurted out. He would come back for the milk later. Turning his back on Olivia's sister, he strode toward the coop. To his annoyance, she trotted along with him.

She continued to chatter questions as if the disturbingly intimate moment back in the barn hadn't happened. How many chickens did they have? What breeds were they? How many eggs a day did they gather? Did they sell the surplus eggs?

Andrew answered in monosyllables as he fed and watered the poultry, stuffed a few late eggs into one of several baskets Olivia always kept in the coop, and finally emerged from the small building and latched the door behind him. He couldn't wait to shake himself of Adele's clinginess.

Finally, as it was growing dusky, he entered the house with Adele hot on his heels.

"Olivia?" he called, anxious to dilute Adele's presence.

No answer.

Frowning, he peeked out the back door, wondering if she was out in the garden for some reason. But she wasn't. She had not lit a lamp against the increasing darkness, as she always did. She wasn't in her studio, or her bedroom, or any of the other rooms. And Helen was nowhere to be seen either.

"She's gone," he said in a shocked voice. He suddenly felt lost and alone. The natural coziness and domesticity Olivia's mere presence lent to the house was absent. His hands shook as he struck a match and lit a kerosene lamp.

"Gone where?" Adele asked in mild surprise.

"I don't know. She didn't say anything." His eyes narrowed as he glanced at Adele. "Could she be avoiding you?"

Adele tossed her head. "Maybe. She's done it before. Why is it so important if she's gone? And why would a handsome man like yourself even look twice at someone like Olivia?"

Andrew clenched his hands into fists. As a man schooled in pacificism since infancy, he rarely felt a desire to be violent with anyone. But he had to discipline himself to control his rage at the utter idiocy and cluelessness of his sister-in-law.

"Because Olivia is my wife," he told her furiously. "We had a small private ceremony a few weeks ago, and we're having a proper church wedding in November."

To her credit, Adele looked shocked at this information. "I didn't know..." she whispered. "No one told me..."

"Well, now you do. And for that reason, Adele, you need to keep your hands and your comments to yourself. I won't have you slander my wife."

"But I thought she was your business partner!" she half wailed. "No one told me you were married!"

"Because we *are* business partners. But our relationship has gone beyond that. Not that it's any of your business," he growled. He was unable to resist adding, "I don't think I've ever seen such a contrast between sisters." In the back of his mind was deep concern about where Olivia and Helen had gone, especially at this time of evening.

"We've always been different." Adele looked like she had recovered from the shock of his announcement. "But it's only because she knows men prefer me over her." Her eyes took on a sultry expression in the lamplight. "I can make you forget her, Andrew…"

He spun Adele around by the shoulders and shoved her toward the door, nudging her strongly to push her forward. "I want you out of this house and off the property, now!"

"Wait!" she wailed. "I have nowhere to go!"

"I don't care. I want you gone. You've crossed every boundary and chased Olivia away from her own home. You must leave."

"But I'm serious!" she cried, her face crumpling. She looked at him tearfully. "I have no place to go!"

"I don't care. I want you gone."

"But Olivia always takes me in!"

"Not this time. Your own actions chased her away, and if you think I'm going to let you stay—especially without her here—you have another thing coming. There's a boardinghouse in town where you can find a room. Now, out, out, out!" He literally shoved her out the front door, slammed it behind her and locked it. Then he strode across the darkened house and locked the back door.

He blew out the oil lamp, and in the darkened house, he looked out the window. He saw Adele standing on the front porch, looking out over the shadowed lawn, her shoulders drooping. After a long pause, looking defeated, she finally descended the porch steps, moving like an old woman. She walked down the driveway and disappeared through the tunnel of trees toward the road.

Did she really have no place to go? Andrew didn't know, and at the moment he was too furious to care. It was a long walk to town, and he prayed it would give her an opportunity to repent of her sins.

Meanwhile, he had to find Olivia and Helen. Because one thing was certain: if he had any doubts about his feelings for Olivia before, they were gone. He loved her. He was sure of that beyond a shadow of a doubt. Her stalwart presence made this house a home, and her motherly air allowed little Helen to thrive under her care.

He waited until he was certain Adele was gone. Then he lit a hurricane lamp and carried it toward the barn. There he lit the carriage lamps on either side of the buggy, hitched up Maggie the horse and directed the animal out of the barn.

He had to find his wife...and his daughter. They were more important than anything else—including the farm.

Chapter Fifteen

Olivia was exhausted by the time she reached the rental cabin. It was almost dark, and her arms were tired from carrying both the baby and the basket of necessities. She'd had to stop and rest once or twice. She considered it a blessing that she had met no one on the road. Right now she didn't feel like explaining why she was wandering about this late in the evening.

Was this flight from humiliation worth it? Yes. All it took was the memory of how Andrew had looked at Adele to know she had to get out of there.

All her life, it had been this way, with men flocking around Adele like moths to a flame. But this time it was worse. This time it was the man she loved who suddenly had eyes for no one else except her glamorous sister.

The thing was, she knew the kind of tantalizing net her sister could weave. It was easy for men to be ensnared—at least at first—but over and over, the men she captured had grown tired of her company after a few months, or a year or two at most. Then Adele would come slinking back to her childhood home, seeking the sensible, no-nonsense lifestyle of her younger sister.

But now there was no childhood home. With her father dead and Olivia relocated to Montana, what was there for Adele to come back to?

A thin trickle of pity for her sister filtered through Olivia's veins. But it was rapidly extinguished by the knowledge that even now, Adele was unabashedly throwing herself at the man she, Olivia, loved.

The bishop had suggested she pray for Adele—pray for her sister's redemption. It had been a long time since she had honestly, sincerely prayed for her only sibling. And even now, her prayer held more of a note of desperation: *Dear Gott, please don't let her take Andrew away from me...*

She trudged up to the front door of the dark rental cabin. While it held the barest of furnishings—a bed, a table, two kitchen chairs, a rocking chair—she had no bed linens, no lamps, no food, no comforts of any sort. It was merely a roof over her head for the night.

With a sigh, she placed the basket on the floor and removed Helen from the sling. The baby had fallen asleep during the journey, and in the dim light coming in through the windows, she made up a bottle of formula she knew would be required after she changed the infant's diaper.

She was glad to have the baby with her, glad to have anything she could love and cuddle and seek comfort from. She felt as if Helen was a sort of lifeline—not so much to her sister, as to Andrew.

She wondered how long he would be hers, now that Adele was on the scene.

Tomorrow she would figure out what to do. No matter how much Andrew might dither around with his interest in Adele, Olivia was still linked to him financially.

What could she do about that? Nothing. Who could buy her out? No one. No one would want half interest in a farm they couldn't fully own. Olivia changed Helen's diaper, then slumped down in the rocking chair as the baby gulped the formula. Would she have to kiss her inheritance goodbye? Should she move in to another Amish community?

Her thoughts flip-flopped first one way, then another. She honestly didn't know what to do. And every time her mind darted toward the vision of Andrew and Adele, arms linked, on their way to the barn, she jerked her thoughts away. It was far too painful a vision.

Helen finished her bottle, and Olivia tossed a clean diaper over her shoulder and raised the baby up to burp her.

Rocking slowly in the dark room, with the infant in her arms, she gave in to her weariness and closed her eyes. Without meaning to, she drifted to sleep.

Then she had a dream. In the dream, Adele stood in front of her, weeping piteously, lamenting her choices in life.

"I'm backed into a corner," her dream sister wept. "I've spent my whole life depending on my looks to get by, and what do I have to show for it? Nothing. I have no home, no skills, no husband, and my only child is being raised by my sister. Oh, what have I done?"

Olivia was conscious of a piercing sense of pity. She told Adele, "Come back. Come back to the church. It's the only way you'll be happy."

"I can't," the dream Adele cried. "No one would want me. I would be an outcast."

"No one is an outcast if they truly want to change," she replied. "But you have to *want* to change…"

"Help me," begged Adele. "Help me to change."

"I will help you," promised Olivia, and even her dream self was aware of a sense of weariness and futility at the offer.

An owl hooted nearby, and Olivia woke up with a start. The dream lingered, vivid and disturbing. Could her sister ever change? Would she ever want to? Olivia had seen absolutely no indication that Adele had ever regretted her choices in life, as appalling as those choices were.

But—and this was a disturbing thought—would she help Adele if asked?

No. Not after stealing away her man. It was out of the question. Adele was on her own, and Olivia at last had run out of patience with her older sister's recalcitrant lifestyle.

But the unease lingered. Was *Gott* trying to tell her something? Why would she dream such a dream?

Helen stirred against her shoulder, and Olivia focused on the child. This baby, her beloved father's long-awaited grandchild, would become Olivia's priority. She was innocent of her mother's sins, and Olivia intended for the infant to grow up in the faith, learning the skills necessary to make her a productive member of society. She would not let Helen grow up to be like her mother. She would not.

She raised her head and listened. Faintly, in the distance, she heard a clip-clop of horse hooves on gravel. For some reason her heart gave a little jump. It was not normal for horses to be driven after dark, even with the required presence of carriage lamps. Most people found it safer and easier to conclude their business before nightfall, then stay at home after dark. Who could be driving out this late?

She rose from the rocking chair and peered out the front window. She could see nothing yet—but then, carriage lamps were not very bright and wouldn't shine very far. She waited, heart beating fast, until a dark shape with two spots of light became visible a distance down the road. Doubtless, it was just someone out for a late-night errand. It couldn't possibly be Andrew.

Yet the horse slowed and turned up the short driveway straight toward the rental cabin. Olivia's heart leaped. With the baby still on her shoulder, she moved to the front door and stepped out onto the small porch, waiting.

Andrew pulled the horse to a stop in front of the building. There was a brief silence as she met his eyes in the dim light of the carriage lamps.

"Come home," he said in a pleading voice.

"Nein," she replied. "You made it clear which of us you prefer. I wanted to preserve some of my dignity, so I left."

"I made nothing clear," he replied, and there was a note of anger in his voice. "But Adele's gone. I kicked her out of the house and then came in search of you. *Bitte*, Olivia, come home."

"Gone? Gone where? Where did she go?" She was momentarily bewildered by the abrupt change of circumstance.

"I don't know and I don't care. I told her there

was a boardinghouse in town and she could get a room there. But I wasn't about to have that woman in the house one minute longer, especially without you there."

"Why?"

He met her eyes gravely. "Isn't it obvious?"

"Nein," she said harshly. "It's always been the same story. Whenever my sister is on the scene, no one can see me. You're just the latest in a long line of people who have acted the same way. It's been nothing but a long and painful series of episodes in my life."

"You saw me trying to be polite to my sister-in-law," he said grimly. "And it didn't work. That's why I kicked her out. *Bitte*, Olivia, come home. You and Helen. You don't belong here, you belong on the farm. With me."

She wanted to. Oh, how she wanted to. She was suddenly bone weary, and desperately yearned for the solid, stable life she and Andrew had been building before this day's interruption. Besides, there was nothing here in the rental cabin beyond the pathetic basket of mostly baby supplies she had packed. She sighed. "Wait a moment for me to get my things."

Mostly by way of groping in the dark room, she located the basket and stashed the diaper supplies, baby bottle and can of powdered formula back inside. Then she slipped Helen into the sling, picked up the basket and stepped back out onto the porch, closing the door behind her.

"Let me have the basket." Andrew took the container and settled it behind the seat. "And I'll take the baby."

Olivia nodded, slipped Helen out of the sling and handed her up to Andrew. He settled the baby in the travel basket the child was accustomed to, which was routinely kept in the buggy.

He extended a hand, and she clasped it and climbed into the buggy, settling on the seat with Helen between them. Then, without warning, Andrew yanked her into his arms and kissed her, long and deep.

He'd wanted to do this forever, and kissing Olivia felt even better than he ever imagined. If he'd had any doubts about her feelings for him, they were swept away as he felt her response.

Finally, he broke away. "If only Helen weren't here," he growled, gesturing at the travel basket on the seat between them.

She laughed shakily. "I'm glad she's here or things might get carried away. Andrew...you're sure you wouldn't rather be with my sister?"

"Your *sister*? *Nein!*" He frowned. "Though, until I met her, I didn't have a clear understanding why you're infinitely preferable to anyone else I've ever known. Olivia, I love you. This won't be a marriage of convenience come November—at least on my part."

"Oh, on my part t-too." Her voice still shook. "I was beyond heartbroken at the thought of losing you. Th-that's why I left. I couldn't bear to watch Adele working her charms on you."

"She tried. I'll admit, she tried. But all I could see was Sarah pulling my strings like a puppet and how false it all became in the end. Whatever beauty Adele has just turned to dust in my eyes once I recognized the similarities." He wiped a hand over his face. "Truth be told, I felt almost...almost unclean around her. I'm sorry, I know she's your sister, but I didn't like being in the same place as her."

"I d-don't know whether to be happy or sorry for her. Maybe both."

"It's okay to feel both. She's your sister, after all, for good or for bad. But having met her, it wasn't hard for me to decide which sister is worth her weight in gold."

"Oh, Andrew...you say the nicest things." Her eyes shimmered with tears, barely visible in the light from the carriage lamps.

"I say the truth. Now..." He turned and picked up the reins. "Let's go home."

Home. He knew now the farm wouldn't be worth the money he'd put into it without Olivia there. She brought comfort and joy to the property, along with the baby she'd taken in.

"I always longed for a family," he mused out loud. "I think that's one of the reasons I was so shattered by Sarah's departure. She didn't just leave me high and dry—she took away any hope for the family I wanted. With you and Helen, it's like a built-in family, and I can't tell you how empty the house is without you both there."

"I'm kind of the opposite," Olivia said. "I never expected to have a family at all. Besides the fact that she's my *daed's* only granddaughter, I think that's why I was so anxious to keep Helen. What hope did I have for children of my own? None. No man had ever even looked twice at me."

"Then they were all fools," he said gruffly. He reached across the baby's basket and seized her hand, feeling her fingers lace through his. "They overlooked the brightest jewel in the treasure chest. But that's okay. *Gott* was keeping you for me, and I'm selfish enough to never let you go."

Olivia sniffed, as if fighting back tears, but didn't say much until he withdrew his hand from hers so he could guide the horse down their driveway.

The house was dark. Andrew pulled the buggy up in front of the lawn gate and said, "Go on in. I'll stable the horse."

"Ja, gut." She climbed down from the buggy, and he handed down the baby and the basket of supplies.

He guided Maggie into the barn and unhitched her from the buggy. He kissed the horse's nose in gratitude, then gave her a few oats as a reward after stabling her. He blew out the carriage lamps and, by dint of starlight, made his way toward the house, where already a light was shining.

He found Olivia changing Helen's diaper by lamplight. A bottle of formula was standing ready on the counter. He took a moment to savor the scene and appreciate the tall, lanky woman, who smiled at him in the warm glow of the lamp. "She was wet. I'm surprised she didn't fuss during all this drama."

"I can't tell you how happy I am to have you both back. Do you want me to feed her?" he asked as she lifted the clean baby off the changing table.

"Nein, I'll do it." She snatched up the bottle and went to sit in the rocking chair. Helen stayed quiet as she began to feed. "I have a feeling she'll be asleep in a little while anyway."

"Gut. Then we can talk." Andrew drew another chair close by. "First, I owe you an apology. I did not mean to give the wrong impression upon meeting Adele. It's just that…"

"That she tends to overwhelm." Olivia smiled

at him. "I understand how that works. I *more* than understand." Her smile faltered. "But when it happened to the man I love…"

"Now, those are words I longed to hear." It seemed almost too good to be true, in fact. "But truth be told, aside from just trying to be polite to my sister-in-law, I was disillusioned even before you came home."

"What clued you in?" she asked. "I'm serious. Most men take a long time to discover what she's like under that beautiful facade."

"I was a little rude," he admitted. "I told her it was a rotten thing to abandon her own child. She kind of laughed it off and said she didn't abandon Helen, she just thought you, as her aunt, might like to get to know her."

Olivia made a shocked noise. "That's a lie…" she whispered.

"*Ja*, a very blatant lie. I mean, I was on the scene within minutes after you found Helen on your doorstep. I know what happened. I also know what *could* have happened, say, if you hadn't been home or something. Helen would have been all alone for who knows how long." He gave a small shudder at the thought. "In that instant, whatever physical attraction Adele had just turned ugly in my eyes. It's like blinders were stripped off."

"Now that…now that I have you," said Olivia,

the quiver back in her voice, "I can almost find it in my heart to feel sorry for her. I was less than charitable in my thoughts an hour ago," she added more fiercely. "But everything's changed now."

"Everything's changed and nothing's changed," he replied. "I'm so grateful to *Gott* for putting that crazy idea into my head to ask if you wanted to buy the farm with me." He smiled at her. "I had no idea I'd be partnering with my future wife—and not just a business wife, but a real one." The idea of loving Olivia still filled him with awe.

"We may still have to deal with Adele," warned Olivia. "She made noises like she was going to take Helen back, but I told her I would take her to court if she did. I'm glad you advised me to keep that note she left. It's solid proof of abandonment."

"She may also still be in town," he warned. "When she said she had nowhere to go and I mentioned the boardinghouse, I have no idea if she went there or not. But I can't imagine she left town, not this late at night. It's not like Pierce has a lot of public transportation options."

"I wonder how she got here to begin with?" mused Olivia. "To the best of my knowledge, she doesn't own a car." She sighed. "I nodded off a while ago, while still in the rental cabin. I had a dream that Adele was crying and lamenting her life choices and begging for help. I told her she should come back to the church, and she said she couldn't, that she would be an outcast. I promised her I'd help her change. That's when I woke up." She shuddered. "It was a very vivid dream."

"Would you?" he asked curiously. "If she truly wanted to change, would you help her?"

Olivia hesitated. *"Ja,"* she said at last. "I know my *daed* would want me to. And *Gott* would want me to also. But she has to *want* to change. Up to this point, I've never seen her make an effort."

"But enough about Adele," Andrew stated. "I'd rather talk about us."

"Suddenly, I find myself wishing Helen would finish feeding so I can put her down to sleep." Olivia gave him a shy smile.

"Ja, me too," he croaked. "I know technically we're married, and I promised to keep things platonic between us, but…well, courting couples are allowed some license, after all."

"So *are* we courting?" It was the closest he'd ever heard to a flirtatious tone in her voice, and he liked it immensely.

"Ja! A thousand times, *ja!* Is the baby finished yet?"

She chuckled. "I'm guessing she'll be finished and ready to sleep in about ten minutes."

At long last, Helen dropped off to sleep. Olivia slipped the bottle out of the baby's mouth, rose and disappeared into her bedroom to put the infant in the basket-cradle on the floor beside her bed. Andrew waited impatiently for her to finish.

When she finally emerged, he took her hand. "Come here." He slipped his arms around her waist and felt her arms snake around his neck. For a moment all he did was hug her. It felt so good to have her in his arms after such a long business association but no personal connection.

"I love you," he whispered, dipping his head for a kiss.

Chapter Sixteen

"We still need to decide what to do about Adele." Olivia gently played with Helen's feet as the infant sat in her bouncy seat in the center of the table.

The morning sunshine poured through the eastern windows of the log home, making the inside glow with warmth. Glancing around the space, Olivia was conscious of gratitude for what she now had in her life—not just a beautiful farm but also a husband who loved her and a baby to raise.

"I told her she wasn't welcome here," said Andrew, buttering a biscuit. "And while I'm willing to help her if she actually wants to change, that codicil remains. I felt horribly uncomfortable around her, especially without you. I can't risk having her stay with us under any circumstances, not after how she behaved."

"I agree, and I'm not eager to have her here, either, especially since that puts a sort of claim on Helen." Olivia sighed, and some of her giddy elation over Andrew's love faded. "I worry she may push to get Helen back, but I'm serious about taking her to court if she tries. But what if she stays in town? As Helen gets older, will she learn Adele is her real mother?"

"Don't borrow trouble," Andrew advised. "We'll cross that bridge when we come to it."

"I still have so many questions," Olivia mused. "How did she return to Pierce? Did someone drop her off? Did she take the bus? Does she own a car? Does she have any suitcases or other possessions with her? If she told you she has no place to go, part of me worries she's absolutely destitute. It might be one of the few times she doesn't have a man to provide for her, and I worry she doesn't know how to provide for herself."

"Do you want to take the buggy into town and see if she made it to the boardinghouse?"

"Ja," she answered slowly. "I might. I don't know why, but I feel strongly that I should follow up with her today."

"I can watch Helen while you do, then."

Olivia's heart swelled with love. She knew Andrew didn't share her concerns about her sister, and she couldn't blame him. But he was willing to interrupt his day's work so she could put her mind at ease.

She didn't know why she felt such sudden concern about Adele's well-being except the disturbing dream she had yesterday still lingered, strongly. She wondered if it wasn't a message from *Gott* telling her Adele might still be redeemed.

When she mentioned this to Andrew, he nodded gravely. "I can't dismiss that possibility," he replied. "If *Gott* talks to you, *listen*. I feel strongly it was a message from *Gott* that prompted me to ask if you wanted to buy the farm with me. And look what happened as a result." He smiled at her, a smile of such promise and love that Olivia felt her eyes tear up.

"I can't wait for November," she said softly.

"Neither can I."

An hour later, Olivia hitched up Maggie to the buggy and headed into town. She stopped at the boardinghouse and inquired of Mathew Miller, the proprietor, whether Adele was within.

"Ja!" he exclaimed. "She came in late yesterday evening. Is that your sister?"

"Ja," she admitted. "We've always had a... rocky relationship. But I wanted to talk to her before she left town."

"She's in room 2A," he replied. "As far as I know, she hasn't left."

Heart beating fast, Olivia ascended the stairs to the second floor and knocked on the door. She heard movement within. "Who is it?"

"Olivia."

After a short pause, Adele opened the door. For once, her beauty seemed faded. Her eyes were red-rimmed, as if she'd been crying, and shadowed as if she'd slept badly. Her clothing was rumpled, and Olivia realized she had slept in them.

"You're destitute, aren't you?" she asked flatly.

Adele's shoulders slumped. *"Ja."*

"Meine schwester, how much longer are you going to live like this? Don't you think it's time to turn over a new leaf?"

Adele's face crumpled like a child's, and she began weeping. "I spent my last dollar getting here on the bus yesterday," she choked. "It made me realize how much I've depended on you over the years to bail me out whenever I got in trouble. I don't even know how I'm going to pay for this room..."

"Inside. Get inside." Olivia gave Adele a small push back into the room and followed, closing the door behind her. "We need to talk. First of all, Andrew has made it clear you are not welcome to stay on the farm. Not after the way you behaved toward him yesterday."

Adele looked, if possible, even more defeated. "I understand. And I owe him—and you—a huge apology for my behavior."

"In some ways, I don't think you could help

yourself." Olivia spoke with more assurance now that she was confident of Andrew's love. "You spent your whole life depending on your looks to get by. But Adele, looks fade. You're thirty-three years old. When are you going to learn to stand on your own two feet?"

"Now."

The admission caught Olivia by surprise, and she interrupted her scolding. "Now?"

"Now."

Olivia blinked. Was her dream playing out in reality?

"I can't tell you how jealous I was when I saw your place yesterday," Adele went on. "You have everything. I have nothing. I don't even have my baby anymore. And I can't blame anyone but myself." The tears flowed afresh. "As you say, I'm thirty-three years old. When Jake—that's the guy I went to Europe with—dumped me for a pretty Dutch woman, I realized I'm getting too old to keep sugar daddies. Yet I've never, as you put it, stood on my own two feet before. How can I learn now?"

The pity for her sister was renewed. For better or worse, Adele was her only blood relative. "Have you thought about returning to the church?" she asked gently.

"Nein!" Adele cried. "I've done too many bad things in my life. Who would want me?"

"Outcast," Olivia murmured, recalling her dream.

"*Ja,*" Adele replied. "I would be an outcast."

"It depends," Olivia replied, "on if you're really willing to change or if this is just another ruse for pity. I've known you for a long time," she added sternly. "You've made promises before about changing, and you've gone straight back to your old escapades."

"*Ja,* I know I have." Adele snatched up a handkerchief from the bedside table and blew her nose. "So how can I prove it?"

Olivia sighed. "You could start by finding a job. I know a store where they're looking for a baker. You were always *gut* at making breads and such. Why don't you apply there?"

For the first time, Olivia saw hope—genuine hope—on her sister's face, before she once again slumped down. "Would they hire me without references?" she faltered.

"The owners of the store are Amish," Olivia replied. "And they're *gut* business people. If I vouch for you, I have a feeling they'll give you a chance. But if I vouch for you," she added sternly, "you'd better not mess up. If you do—if you flake out or stop going to work or try to latch up with another man—then I will wash my hands of you. I certainly won't take in any more babies you produce. You've spent your whole life making bad choices, Adele. Here's your opportunity to turn over a new leaf. Make the most of it."

"What about a place to stay?" sniffed her sister.

She thought for a moment. "You could stay in the little rental cabin I was living in when you dropped Helen on my doorstep. It's vacant and partially furnished."

The faint gleam of hope was back on Adele's face. Watching the play of emotions, Olivia had a revelation about her sister: it seemed that, despite her beauty, she utterly lacked self-confidence.

"I'll try it," Adele said softly.

Olivia nodded. "I'll go talk to the store owners and see if they're interested. Meanwhile, if I were you, I'd clean up a bit." Olivia rose, then turned. "And, Adele—heed my advice. *Leave the men alone.* Stay single for a while. You need to learn to love yourself before you can expect any man to love you for more than a few weeks. Do I make myself clear?"

"*Ja.* I promise you. Olivia… One more thing. Where can I get an Amish dress and *kapp*?"

Olivia stared. "Why? You're not Amish."

"*Nein*, I'm not. But if I'm going to start attending church services, I don't want to be dressed like this." She plucked at her wrinkled blouse and skirt.

Olivia softened. If there was even the smallest chance her sister could be redeemed, she had to help. "I'll talk to a woman I know who's clever with sewing. I'm sure she can pull something together for you. I'll also talk to the owners of the rental cabin. Meanwhile, if you want to attend church, I suggest you start by having a meeting with the bishop. He can guide you far better than I can."

A look of dread crept into Adele's eyes. "He'll want a full confession. That's not going to be easy."

"Did you expect it to be? But it's a step. Adele, you're three years older than me, but right now I feel like your mother. Don't mess things up." She leaned down and kissed her sister on the cheek. "I'm leaving now. I have some people to talk to."

It was hours before Olivia returned home, and Andrew found himself impatient—not just to see her, but to find out what was taking her so long.

At long last, he heard the clip-clop of hooves coming up the driveway, and he stepped out on the porch—Helen on his hip—to see Maggie emerge from the tunnel of trees with Olivia at the reins. Adele, to his relief, was not with her, as he'd half expected her to be. Olivia smiled and waved, then drove directly to the barn.

He went inside and put water on to boil for tea. He had a feeling she had a lot to tell him.

He put the baby on a blanket on the floor since the infant enjoyed practicing lifting her head.

The moment Olivia stepped inside, he swept her into an embrace. Now that he knew such advances wouldn't be rejected, he was eager to apply them. "You were gone a lot longer than I thought you'd be."

"*Ja.* What a morning." She kissed him, then slipped out of his arms. "I think you kicking Adele out yesterday was the best thing that ever happened to her."

"It was?" His voice scaled up in surprise.

"It scared her," she replied. The kettle started to steam, so she moved into the kitchen and began assembling the tea things. "She's effectively destitute and says she's ready to turn over a new leaf. I have my doubts it will stick, so I gave her some advice she must follow, and made it clear if she didn't follow through, I would utterly wash my hands of her. *And* I wouldn't take in any more of her babies."

"What kind of advice?"

"Get a job, stick with it and—most importantly—stay away from men. *All* men. She also sounded like she might be interested in returning to the church, and for that she'll have to have a long talk with the bishop since that's his call, not mine."

He gave a whistle. "Whew. That's a lot. Do you think it will work?"

She turned the heat off under the kettle and poured boiling water into two mugs. "For the first time in my life, I'm hopeful. First, I went and talked to Abe and Mabel Yoder. They've hired a baker, though he's still back east and hasn't moved out here yet. Mabel said they were interested in hiring an assistant for him. Adele is a *gut* baker. Or used to be. I'm sure she could pick it up again. I explained the circumstances around Adele and outlined my conditions regarding my sister, and they agreed to give her a try. Then I went to see Anna Miller about having Adele rent the cabin, and she agreed. Lastly, I went to see Eva Hostetler about sewing a dress and apron, since Adele says she wants to dress properly. Then I went back to see Adele and told her everything I did on her behalf."

Andrew stared at his wife. He knew she had a spine of steel, but this was the first time he'd seen it in action. Somehow her firm determination made her even more attractive in his eyes. "How did she react?"

"She seemed grateful. Actually, she seemed *pathetically* grateful. She said as soon as Eva has her clothes ready, she'll go see the Yoders. Then I took her to the grocery store and bought her some food she could keep in her room, paid for a few days at the boardinghouse and finally came home. Oh, and I warned her she was never to darken the doorway of this house until you explicitly give her permission." She gave him an impish grin.

"*Danke* for that," he said. "Wow. No wonder you were gone so long. While I'm not eager to see your sister anytime soon, I pray she follows your advice."

"Me too. I—I had to try, Andrew. I had to try and redeem her for *Daed's* sake. He spent his whole life regretting the way Adele turned out, and I know he blamed himself. I suppose you could say this is my last gift to my *vader*."

Helen made a gurgling noise, and Andrew got the impression she wanted to be held. He picked her up and settled the baby in his lap.

A thought struck him. "If Adele stays in town, what about Helen?"

"Helen stays with us."

"But what about when she gets older? It's no secret in the community that Adele is her birth mother. What will we tell Helen when she's old enough to understand?"

"Oh." Olivia frowned and put her mug of tea back on the table. She thought for a few moments. "I suppose we'll just have to be truthful about it. We can address Adele as her *tante*, and say *Tante* Adele couldn't take care of you when you were born, so your *daed* and I stepped in to bring you up. Something like that."

"Her *daed*." He gave the baby a little bounce. "I like that title."

"I only hope Helen doesn't grow up to be rebellious as Adele did," Olivia sighed. "She shows promise of being just as beautiful as her mother ever was."

Andrew gave a slow smile. "You know what? Maybe it's *gut* Adele will be here as Helen grows up. If she reaches a stage where she becomes rebellious, her birth mother can step in and tell her what life is like in the big wide world. It might scare her straight, so to speak."

Olivia's face cleared. "Maybe so." She gave a rueful chuckle. "I told you once before that Helen and I stood to benefit more from this marriage of convenience than you did. Are you sure you don't have regrets? I'm bringing a lot of baggage with me."

"If propriety wasn't in the way," he told her seriously, "I'd prove to you just how satisfied I am with this marriage. It's no longer a business arrangement, Olivia. It's a love match. At least on my part," he added with just a thread of uncertainty.

That uncertainty vanished in an instant. "On both our parts," she told him. She held out her hand on the tabletop, and he threaded his fingers through hers. "I never thought I would be married, much less married to the kindest and best-looking man I know."

"What a pity the Shrocks didn't plant any celery," he teased. "It's too late to plant it now, and I have a feeling we'll need a lot at our official wedding." Celery had a rich and nuanced meaning at Amish weddings. Not only was it often the only plant still showing leafy greenery during November, but its presence hinted subtly at fertility.

She chuckled. "I don't think we'll have any trouble finding someone growing celery. Maybe even the bishop or his wife."

"*Gott* has a sense of humor, of that I'm sure," Andrew said. "Considering the bizarre circumstances under which we got together, what other explanation is there?"

She tightened her fingers in his. "Whatever the explanation, I know *Gott ist gut*."

Epilogue

The early November day dawned rainy and gray, but nothing could dampen Olivia's mood. She stood against a wall. Vases of leafy celery adorned the tables set up in the spacious lobby of Miller's Boardinghouse in town. The room was crowded with the cheerful chatter that followed a wedding ceremony.

She watched two people. Andrew, now fully her husband, talked with some visiting relatives. His face was animated, and occasionally he looked her way with absolute love in his eyes. She felt herself soften whenever their glances met.

And Adele, outfitted demurely in proper Amish clothing, held Helen in her lap while chatting with Lois Beiler. The last two months had brought about such astounding changes in her sister that Olivia still couldn't quite believe it. *Gott* was indeed *gut*.

"What are you thinking about?" murmured Andrew in her ear.

"I didn't hear you come up," she replied. She turned and smiled at him. "Just thinking how happy I am. Adele seems to be straightening out, she's on *gut* terms with Helen while not overstepping any boundaries—and most of all, I'm now really and truly your wife." She resisted the urge to slip her arms around his waist. In the crowded room, such displays of affection would be noticed instantly.

He dropped a quick kiss on her nose. "I wonder if Helen can stay with Adele for just one night."

"No, she can't," she gently scolded with a smile. "Besides, Helen has been sleeping well now. She's on a schedule."

"Gut." He gave her a mischievous smile.

"Andrew..." she said in a warning tone, but she felt butterflies in her midsection.

He was always like this now—affectionate and playful, teasing and joyous. Olivia still had a hard time believing that she—tall and plain, gawky and angular—had been given the privilege of marrying such an incredible man. In addition to her wedding vows, she silently promised *Gott* she would be the best wife she could be.

The wet weather meant wedding guests couldn't spill outside during the reception, and Olivia knew every room in the boardinghouse was full with out-of-town relatives. But somehow the joyous hubbub filled her heart with elation. Despite the brief experience of cold shoulders when she and Andrew first started sharing the farm, everyone had come to understand the circumstances and warmed up. And now...well, this was her church now.

And this—she turned to Andrew—was her *hutband*. *Gott* was indeed *gut*.

*****

Dear Reader,

Sometimes a book starts with an idea rather than a character. In this case, I wanted to write a marriage-of-convenience story, and wondered how I could make it work in the modern day. Thus Olivia and Andrew were born, and I worked the story backward.

While writing Olivia and Andrew's story, I managed to add many things dear to my heart: a beautiful farm, a baby named Helen (which was my grandmother's name), and a secondary character who's redeemed (you might even see her in a future book!). This, dear reader, is why writing for Love Inspired is so enjoyable.

I love hearing from readers, so feel free to email me at patricelewis@protonmail.com.

Blessings,
Patrice

Harlequin Reader Service

Enjoyed your book?

Try the perfect subscription for Romance readers and get more great books like this delivered right to your door.

See why over 10+ million readers have tried Harlequin Reader Service.

Start with a Free Welcome Collection with free books and a gift—valued over $20.

Choose any series in print or ebook.
See website for details and order today:

TryReaderService.com/subscriptions